She didn't need protecting from the elements. She needed protection from *him*. Or was it herself? She was no longer sure.

Confused and jittery, Avery parked and sprang from the vehicle. "You can camp by that rock and I'll camp by the other." Distance, she thought. She needed distance. They needn't even see each other until morning. She'd zip her tent up and she'd keep it zipped.

"There is just one tent, Avery."

"What?" His words blew out the foundations of her fledgling plan and answered any remaining questions she had about her feelings for him. "Just one!"

"I don't intend to sleep with you." He leaned in and pulled a bag from the vehicle. "Just share a tent with you. It isn't as if we haven't done it before."

But the last time they'd been lovers. Intimate in every way.

He'd be sleeping with his head next to hers. His body within touching distance.

**The Private Lives of
PUBLIC PLAYBOYS**

*Two notorious billionaires with
one unbreakable rule:*

work hard...and play harder!

Billionaire tycoon Lucas Jackson is no stranger to business deals conducted in the desert—but it's the snowstorm whirling around his English country estate that most closely resembles his ice-cold heart!

Sheikh Malik rules the Kingdom of Zubran, and has never met anyone who didn't bow to his command. Until now...

Both are infamous worldwide for having the Midas touch in the boardroom...and a decadently sinful touch in the bedroom.

Last month you read Lucas Jackson's story in

A NIGHT OF NO RETURN

This month Sheikh Malik needs a queen for his desert kingdom!

WOMAN IN A SHEIKH'S WORLD

Sarah Morgan

WOMAN IN A
SHEIKH'S WORLD

The Private Lives of
PUBLIC PLAYBOYS

HARLEQUIN®
entertain, enrich, inspire™

Recycling programs
for this product may
not exist in your area.

ISBN-13: 978-0-373-13110-5

WOMAN IN A SHEIKH'S WORLD

Copyright © 2012 by Sarah Morgan

www.Harlequin.com

Printed in U.S.A.

All about the author…
Sarah Morgan

USA TODAY bestselling author **SARAH MORGAN** writes lively, sexy stories for both Harlequin Presents® and Medical Romance.

As a child Sarah dreamed of being a writer, and although she took a few interesting detours on the way, she is now living that dream. With her writing career she has successfully combined business with pleasure and she firmly believes that reading romance is one of the most satisfying and fat-free escapist pleasures available. Her stories are unashamedly optimistic and she is always pleased when she receives letters from readers saying that her books have helped them through hard times.

RT Book Reviews has described her writing as "action packed and sexy" and has nominated her books for their Reviewer's Choice Awards and their Top Pick slot.

Sarah lives near London with her husband and two children, who innocently provide an endless supply of authentic dialogue. When she isn't writing or reading Sarah enjoys music, movies and any activity that takes her outdoors.

Readers can find out more about Sarah and her books from her website, www.sarahmorgan.com. She can also be found on Facebook and Twitter.

Other titles by Sarah Morgan available in eBook:

Harlequin Presents®

3068—THE FORBIDDEN FERRARA
3084—DEFYING THE PRINCE *(The Santina Crown)*
3098—A NIGHT OF NO RETURN
         (The Private Lives of Public Playboys)

CHAPTER ONE

SHE dreamed of the desert.

She dreamed of dunes turning red gold under the burning fire of the sun and of the clear blue waters of the Persian Gulf lapping beaches of soft white sand. She dreamed of savage mountains and palm-shaded pools. And she dreamed of a Prince—a Prince with eyes all shades of the night and the power to command armies.

'Avery!' He was calling her name but she carried on walking without looking back. The ground crumbled beneath her feet and she was falling, falling...

'Avery, wake up!'

She rose through clouds of sleep, the voice jarring with the image in her head. It was wrong. *His* voice was rich, deep and everything male. *This* voice was female and amused. 'Mmm?'

The delicious aroma of fresh coffee teased her and she lifted her head and stared at the mug that had been placed next to her on the table. With a groan, she sat up and reached for it, half blind from sleep. 'What time is it?'

'Seven. You were moaning. That must have been some dream.'

Avery pushed her hand through her hair and tried to wake herself up. She had the same dream every night. Thankfully when she woke it was to find herself in

London, not the desert. The discordant blare of taxi horns announced the start of the morning rush hour. No mountains and no shaded oasis—just Jenny, her best friend and business partner, pressing the button on her desk to raise the blinds.

Sunshine poured into the spectacular glass-clad office from all directions and Avery felt a sudden rush of relief to be awake and realise that the ground hadn't crumbled beneath her feet. She hadn't lost everything. This was *hers* and she'd built it from sheer hard work.

'I need to take a quick shower before our meeting.'

'When you ordered this couch for your office, I didn't realise the intention was to sleep on it.' Jenny put her coffee down on Avery's desk and slipped off her shoes. 'Just in case you don't actually know this, I feel it's my duty to point out that normal human beings go home at the end of the working day.'

The disturbing dream clung to Avery's mind like a cobweb and she tried to brush it off, irritated by how much it could affect her. That wasn't her life. *This* was.

Barefoot, she strolled across her office and took a look at her reality.

Through the floor to ceiling windows, the city sparkled in the early morning sunshine, mist wrapping the River Thames in an ethereal cloak as delicate as a bride's veil. Familiar landmarks rose through the milky haze and down on the streets below tiny figures hurried along pavements and cars were already jammed together on the web of roads that criss-crossed beneath her office. Her eyes stung from lack of sleep but she was used to the feeling by now. It had been her close companion for months, along with the empty feeling in her chest that nothing could fill.

Jenny was looking at her. 'Do you want to talk about it?'

'Nothing to talk about.' Avery turned away from the

window and sat down at her desk. *Work,* she thought. Work had been everything until her world had been disturbed. She needed to get that feeling back. 'The good news is that in my extended insomnia moment last night I finished the proposal for the launch in Hong Kong. I've emailed it to you. I think I've excelled myself this time. Everyone is going to be talking about this party.'

'Everyone always talks about your parties.'

The phone she'd left charging overnight buzzed. Back in business mode, Avery reached for it and then saw the name on the screen. Her hand froze in mid-air. *Again?* It was at least the fifth time he'd called.

She couldn't do this now. Not so close to the dream.

Her hand diverted and she switched on her computer instead, her heart thundering like a stampeding herd of wild horses. And layered under the panic was pain. Pain that he could intentionally hurt her like this.

'That's your private number. Why aren't you answering it?' Jenny peered at the screen of the phone and her head jerked up. 'Mal? The Prince is calling you?'

'Apparently.' Avery opened the spreadsheet she'd been working on and noticed with a flash of irritation that her hand wasn't quite steady. 'I should have changed my number.' He had no right to call her private line. She should have cut all ties. Should have made sure he wasn't able to call her except through the office.

'Over' should have meant just that except that he'd made sure that couldn't happen.

'All right, enough. I've ignored what's going on for too long.' Jenny plonked herself down in the chair opposite. 'I'm officially worried about you.'

'Don't be. I'm fine.' The words had been repeated so often they fell out of her mouth on their own. But they didn't convince Jenny.

'The man you loved is marrying another woman. How can you be fine? In your position I'd be screaming, sobbing, eating too much and drinking too much. You're not doing any of those things.'

'Because I didn't love him. We had an affair, that's all. An affair that ended. It happens to people all the time. Shall we get to work now?'

'It was so much more than an affair, Avery. You were in love.'

'Good sex doesn't have to mean love; I don't know why people always think that.' Did she sound calm? *Did she sound as if she didn't care?* Would anyone guess that the numbers on her screen were nonsense? She knew that people were watching her, wondering how she was reacting as the wedding of the Crown Prince drew closer. There were times when she felt like an exhibit in a zoo. It seemed that the whole world was waiting for her to drop to her knees and start sobbing.

And that, she thought, was a shame for them because they were going to be waiting a long time. She'd throw out her stilettos before she'd sob over a man. Especially a man like Mal, who would take such a display of weakness as a sign of another successful conquest. His ego didn't need the boost.

The ringing stopped and then immediately the phone on her desk rang.

Jenny looked at the phone as if it were an enraged scorpion. 'Do you want me to—?'

'No.'

'He's very insistent.'

'He's a Prince—' Avery muted her phone '—he can't help insisting. Mal only has two settings, Prince and General. Either way, he's commanding someone.' No wonder they'd clashed, she thought numbly. No relationship could have two bosses.

There was an urgent tap on the door and Chloe, the new receptionist, virtually fell into the room in her excitement. 'Avery, you'll never guess who is on the phone!' She paused for dramatic effect. 'The Crown Prince of Zubran.' Clearly she expected her announcement to have more impact than it did and when neither of them reacted she repeated herself. 'Did you hear me? *The Crown Prince of Zubran!* I tried to put him through but you weren't picking up.'

'Insistent and persistent,' Jenny murmured. 'You're going to have to answer it.'

'Not right now. Chloe, please tell him I'm unavailable.'

'But it's the Prince himself. Not his assistant or his adviser or anything, but *him*. In person. Complete with melting dark voice and a very cultured accent.'

'Give him my sincere apologies. Tell him I'll call back as soon as I can.' As soon as she'd worked out her strategy. As soon as she was confident she wasn't going to say, or do, something she'd later regret. A conversation like that had to be carefully planned.

Chloe gaped at her. 'You sound so relaxed, like it's normal to have someone like him just calling on the phone. I can't believe you know him. I'd be dropping his name into every conversation. He is so gorgeous,' she confessed in a breathy voice. 'Not just in the obvious way, although I wouldn't object if he wanted to take his shirt off and chop wood in front of me or something, but because he's just such a *man* if you know what I mean. He's tough in a way men aren't allowed to be any more because it's not considered politically correct. You just know he is not the sort to ask permission before he kisses you.'

Avery looked at their newly appointed receptionist and realised with surprise that the girl didn't know. Chloe was one of the few people not to know that Avery Scott had once had a wild and very public affair with Crown Prince Malik of Zubran.

She thought about the first time he'd kissed her. No, he hadn't asked permission. The Prince didn't ask permission for anything. For a while she'd found it exhilarating to be with a man who wasn't intimidated by her confidence and success. Then she'd realised that two such strong people in a relationship was a recipe for disaster. The Prince thought he knew what was best for everyone. Including her.

Jenny tapped her foot impatiently. 'Chloe, go to the bathroom and stick your head under cold running water. If that doesn't work, try your whole body. Whatever it takes because the Prince is not going to be kissing you any time soon, with or without permission, so you can forget that. Now go and talk to him before he assumes you've passed out or died.'

Chloe looked confused. 'But what if it's something really urgent that can't wait? You *are* arranging his wedding.'

Wedding.

The word sliced into Avery like a blade through soft flesh, the pain taking her by surprise. 'I'm not arranging his wedding.' The words almost choked her and she didn't understand why. She'd ended their relationship. Her choice. Her decision, freely made. So why did she feel pain that he was marrying another woman? In every way, it was the best possible outcome. 'I'm arranging the evening party and I sincerely doubt that he is calling about that. A Prince does not call to discuss minor details. He won't even know what's in the canapés until he puts them in his mouth. He has staff to deal with details. A Prince has staff to do everything. Someone to drive his car, cook his meals, run his shower—'

'—someone to scrub his back while he's in the shower—' Jenny took over the conversation '—and the reason Avery can't talk to him now is because I need to talk to her urgently about the Senator's party.'

'Oh. The Senator—' Visibly impressed by all the famous names flying around the office, Chloe backed towards the door, her legs endless in skinny jeans, bangles jangling at her wrists. 'Right. But I suspect His Royal Highness is not a man who is good at waiting or being told "no".'

'Then let's give him more practise.' Avery pushed aside memories of the other occasions he'd refused to wait. Like the time he'd stripped her naked with the tip of his ceremonial sword because he couldn't be bothered to unbutton her dress. Or the time he'd…

No, she *definitely* wasn't going to think about *that* one.

As the door closed behind the receptionist, Avery groped for her coffee. 'She's sweet. I like her. Once we've given her some confidence, she'll be lovely. The clients will adore her.'

'She was tactless. I'll speak to her.'

'Don't.'

'Why the hell are you doing this to yourself, Avery?'

'Employing inexperienced graduates? Because everyone deserves a chance. Chloe has lots of raw potential and—'

'I'm not talking about your employment policy, I'm talking about this whole thing with the Prince. What possessed you to agree to arrange your ex's wedding? It is killing you.'

'Not at all. It's not as if I wanted to marry him and anyway I'm not arranging the actual wedding. Why does everyone keep saying I'm arranging his wedding?' A picture of the desert at dawn appeared on her computer and she made a mental note to change her screen saver. Perhaps it was the cause of her recurring dreams. 'I'm responsible for the evening party, that's all.'

'*All?* It has the most influential guest list of any party in the last decade.'

'Which is why everything must be perfect. And I don't find it remotely stressful to plan parties. How could I? Parties are happy events populated by happy people.'

'So you really don't care?' Jenny flexed her toes. 'You and the hot Prince were together for a year. And you haven't been out with a man since.'

'Because I've been busy building my business. And it wasn't a year. None of my relationships have lasted a year.'

'Avery, it was a year. Twelve whole months.'

'Oh.' Her heart lurched. A *year?* 'OK, if you say so. Twelve whole months of lust.' It helped her to diminish it. To label it neatly. 'We're both physical people and it was nothing more than sex. I wish people wouldn't romanticize that. It's why so many marriages end in divorce.'

'If it was so incredibly amazing, why did you break up?'

Avery felt her chest tighten. She didn't want to think about it. 'He wants to get married. I don't want to get married. I ended it because it had no future.' *And because he'd been arrogant and manipulative.* 'I'm not interested in marriage.'

'So these dreams you're having don't have anything to do with you imagining him with his virgin princess?'

'Of course not.' Avery reached into her bag and pulled out a packet of indigestion tablets. There were just two left. She needed to buy more.

'You wouldn't need those if you drank less coffee.'

'You're starting to sound like my mother.'

'No, I'm not. No offence intended, but your mother would be saying something like "I can't believe you've got yourself in this state over a man, Avery. This is exactly the sort of thing I warned you about when I taught you at the age of five that you are responsible for every aspect of your life, including your own orgasm.'"

'I was older than five when she taught me that bit.' She chewed the tablet, the ache in her jaw telling her that she'd been grinding her teeth at night again. *Stress.* 'You want to know why I said yes to this piece of business? Because of my pride. Because when Mal called, I was so taken aback that he was getting married so quickly after we broke up, I couldn't think straight.' And she'd been hurt. Horribly, hideously hurt in a way she'd never been hurt before. There was a tight, panicky feeling in her chest that refused to go away. 'He asked if it would feel awkward to arrange the party and I opened my mouth to say *yes, you insensitive bastard, of course it would feel awkward* but my pride spoke instead and under its direction my mouth said no, no of course it won't feel awkward.'

'You need to re-programme your mouth. I've often thought so.'

'Thanks. And then I realised he was probably doing it to punish me because—'

Jenny lifted an eyebrow. 'Because—?'

'Never mind.' Avery, who never blushed, felt herself blushing. 'The truth is, our company is the obvious and right choice for an event like that. If I'd refused, every-one would have been saying, "Of course Avery Scott isn't organising the party because she and the Prince were in-volved and she just can't handle it."' And he would have known. He would have known how much he'd hurt her.

But of course he already knew. And it depressed her to think that their relationship had sunk that low.

'You need to delegate this one, Avery.' Jenny slid her shoes back on. 'You're the toughest, most impressive woman I've ever met but organising the wedding of a man you were once in love with—'

'Was in lust with—'

'Fine, call it whatever you like, but it's making you ill. I've known you since we were both five years old. We've worked together for six years but if you carry on like this I'm going to have to ask you to fire me for the good of my health. The tension is killing me.'

'Sorry.' Out of the corner of her eye Avery noticed that her screen saver was back again. With a rush of irritation she swiftly replaced the desert with a stock picture of the Arctic. 'Talk to me about work. And then I'm going to take a shower and get ready for the day.'

'Ah, work. Senator's golden wedding party. Fussiest client we've ever had—' Jenny flipped open her book and checked through her notes while Avery cupped her mug and took comfort from the warmth.

'Why do you insist on using that book of yours when I provide you with all the latest technology?'

'I like my book. I can doodle and turn clients into cartoons.' Jenny scanned her list. 'He's insisting on fifty swans as a surprise for his wife. Apparently they represent fidelity.'

Avery lowered the mug. 'The guy has had at least three extramarital affairs, one of them extremely public. I don't think this party should be celebrating his "fidelity", do you?'

'No, but I couldn't think of a tactful way to say that when he called me. I'm not you.'

'Then think of one and think of it fast because if he mentions "fidelity" to his wife on the big day we'll have a battlefield, not a party. No swans. Apart from the fidelity connotations they have very uncertain tempers. What else?'

'You want more?' With a sigh, Jenny went back to her notes. 'He wants to release a balloon for each year of their marriage.'

Avery dropped her head onto her desk. 'Kill me now.'

'No, because then I'll have to deal with the Senator alone.'

Reluctantly, Avery lifted her head. 'I don't do balloon releases. And, quite apart from the fact that mass balloon releases are banned in lots of places, isn't our Senator working with some environmental group at the moment? The last thing he needs is publicity like that. Suggest doves. Doves are environmentally friendly and the guests can release them and have a warm, fuzzy eco feeling.' She sat back in her chair, trying to concentrate. 'But not fifty, *obviously*. Two will be fine or the guests will be covered in bird droppings.'

'Two doves.' Jenny made a note in the margin and tapped her pen on the pad. 'He is going to ask me what two doves signify.'

'A lot less mess than fifty swans—OK, sorry, I know you can't say that—let me think—' Avery sipped her coffee. 'Tell him they signify peace and tranquillity. Actually, no, don't tell him that, either. There is no peace and tranquillity in their relationship. Tell him—' She paused, grappling for the right word. *She knew nothing about long-term relationships*. 'Partnership. Yes, that's it. Partnership. The doves signify their life journey together.'

Jenny grinned. 'Which has been full of—'

'Exactly.' With her free hand, Avery closed down the spreadsheet on her computer before she could insert any more errors. 'Take Chloe to help at the Senator's party. We need to cure her of being star-stuck. It will be good experience for her to mingle with celebrities and she can help out if the doves become incontinent.'

'Why don't you let us do the Zubran wedding without you?'

'Because then everyone will say that I can't cope and, worse than that—' she bit her lip '—Mal will think I can't cope.'

Was he still angry with her? He'd been furious, those hooded black eyes as moody as a sky threatening a terrible storm. And she'd been equally angry with him. It had been a clash from which neither of them had pulled back.

Jenny looked at her. 'You miss him, don't you?'

Yes. 'I miss the sex. And the rows.'

'You miss the *rows*?'

Avery caught Jenny's disbelieving glance and shrugged. 'They were mentally stimulating. Mal is super-bright. Some people do crosswords to keep their minds alert. I like a good argument. Comes of having a mother who is a lawyer. We didn't talk at the dinner table, we debated.'

'I know. I still remember the one time you invited me for tea.' Jenny shuddered. 'It was a terrifying experience. But it does explain why you can't admit that you cared for the Prince. Your mother dedicated her life to ending marriages.'

'They were already broken when she got involved.'

Jenny closed her book. 'So this wedding is fine with you? Pride is going to finish you off, you know that, don't you? That and your overachieving personality—another thing I blame your mother for.'

'I *thank* my mother. She made me the woman I am.'

'A raving perfectionist who is truly messed up about men?'

'I won't apologise for wanting to do a job properly and I am not messed up about men. Just because I'm the child of a strong single parent—'

'Avery, I love you, but you're messed up. That one time

I came for tea, your mum was arguing the case for doing away with men altogether. Did she ever even tell you the identity of your father? Did she?'

The feelings came from nowhere. Suddenly she was back in the playground again, surrounded by children who asked too many questions.

Yes, she knew who her father was. And she remembered the night her mother had told her the truth as vividly as if it had happened just yesterday. Remembered the way the strength had oozed from her limbs and the sickness rose in her stomach.

She didn't look at Jenny. 'My father has never been part of my life.'

'Presumably because your mother didn't want him interfering! She scared him away, didn't she?' Jenny was still in full flow. 'The woman is bright as the sun and mad as a bunch of bananas. And don't kid yourself that you had to say yes to this party. You did the launch party for the Zubran Ferrara Spa Resort. That was enough to prove that you're not losing sleep over the Prince.'

The knot in Avery's stomach tightened but part of her was just relieved that the conversation had moved away from the topic of her father. 'There was no reason to say no. I wish Mal nothing but happiness with his virgin princess.' There was a buzzing sound in her head. She *had* to stop talking about Mal. It was doing awful things to her insides. Now she had hearing problems. 'I'm doing the wedding party and then that will be it.' Then everyone would stop speculating that she was broken hearted because of a man. 'You call him, Jen. Tell him I'm out of the country or something. Find out what he wants and sort it out.'

'Does his bride really have to be a virgin?' Jenny sounded curious and Avery felt something twist in her stomach.

'I think she does. Pure. Untouched by human hand. Obedient in all things. His to command.'

Jenny laughed. 'How on earth did you and the Prince ever sustain a relationship?'

'It was…fiery. I'm better at being the commander than the commanded.' The buzzing sound grew louder and she suddenly realised that it wasn't coming from her head, but from outside. 'Someone is using the helipad. We don't have a client flying in today, do we?'

As Jenny shook her head, Avery turned to look, but the helicopter was out of view, landing above her. 'It must be someone visiting one of the other businesses in our building.'

Flanked by armed bodyguards, Mal strode from the helicopter. 'Which floor?'

'Top floor, sir. Executive suite, but—'

'I'll go alone. Wait here for me.'

'But, Your Highness, you can't—'

'It's a party planning company,' Mal drawled, wondering why they couldn't see the irony. 'Who, exactly, is going to threaten my safety in a party planning company? Will I be the victim of a balloon assault? Drowned in champagne? Rest assured, if I encounter danger in the stairwell, I'll deal with it.' Without giving his security guards an opportunity to respond he strode into the building.

Avery had done well for herself since they'd parted company, he thought, and the dull ache that was always with him grew just a little bit more intense as did the anger. She'd chosen this, her business, over their relationship.

But he couldn't allow himself to think about that. He'd long since recognised the gulf between personal wishes and duty. After years pursuing the first, he was now committed to the second. Which was why this visit was professional, not personal.

If he knew Avery as well as he thought he did, then pride would prevent her from throwing him out of her office or slapping his face. He was banking on it. Or maybe she no longer cared enough to do either.

Maybe she'd never cared enough and that was just another thing he'd been wrong about.

Mal passed no one in the stairwell and emerged onto the top floor, through a set of glass doors that guarded the corporate headquarters of Avery Scott's highly successful events planning company, Dance and Dine.

This was the hub of her operation. The nerve centre of an organisation devoted to pleasure but run with military precision. From here, Avery Scott organised parties for the rich and famous. She'd built her business on hard work and sheer nerve, turning down business that wasn't consistent with her vision for her company. As a result of making herself exclusive, her services were so much in demand that a party organized by Avery Scott was often booked years in advance, a status symbol among those able to afford her.

It was the first time he'd visited her offices and he could see instantly that the surroundings reflected the woman. Sleek, contemporary and elegant. A statement of a successful, confident high achiever.

A woman who needed no one.

His mouth tightened.

She certainly hadn't needed him.

The foyer was a glass atrium at the top of the building and light flooded through the glass onto exotic plants and shimmered on low contemporary sofas. A pretty girl sat behind the elegantly curved reception desk, answering the phones as they rang.

For this visit he'd chosen to wear a suit rather than the

more traditional robes but apparently that did nothing to conceal his identity because the moment the receptionist saw him she shot to her feet, panicked and star struck in equal measure.

'Your Highness! You're...ohmigod—'

'*Not* God,' Mal said and then frowned as the colour faded from her cheeks. 'Are you all right?'

'No. I don't think so. I've never met a Prince in the flesh before.' She pressed her hand to her chest and then fanned herself. 'I feel a bit—' She swayed and Mal moved quickly, catching her before she hit the ground.

Torn between exasperation and amusement, he sat her in her chair and pushed her head gently downwards. 'Lean forward. Now breathe. That's it. You'll soon feel better. Can I get you a glass of water?'

'No.' She squeaked the word. 'Thank you for catching me. You're obviously every bit as strong as you look. Hope you didn't put your back out.'

Mal felt a flash of amusement. 'My back is fine.'

'This is seriously embarrassing. I should be curtseying or something, not fainting at your feet.' She lifted her head. 'I presume you're here to see Miss Scott. I don't suppose there is any chance you could not mention this? I'm supposed to be cool with celebrities and famous people. As you can see, it's still a work in progress.'

'My lips are sealed.' Smiling, Mal straightened. 'Sit there and recover. I'll find her myself.' At least the receptionist hadn't pretended her boss wasn't in the building, which was good because his extremely efficient security team had already confirmed that she was here. The fact that she'd refused to pick up the phone had added another couple of coals to his already burning temper but he wasn't about to take that out on this girl. He only fought with people as strong as him and he rarely met anyone who fitted that description.

Fortunately Avery Scott was more than capable of handling anything he dished out. She was the strongest woman he'd ever met. Nothing shook that icy composure. Apparently not even the fact that he was marrying another woman.

Temper held rigidly in control, he strode away from the reception desk and towards the offices and meeting rooms.

Deciding that Avery would choose a corner office with a view, he swiftly calculated the direction of the Thames. There was a large door at the end of the glass atrium and he thrust it open and there, seated behind a large glass desk and talking to another woman was Avery, immaculate as ever, that sheet of shiny blonde hair sliding over a pearl coloured silk shirt.

In those few seconds before she saw him, a tightness gripped his chest.

He felt something he only ever felt around this woman.

As always, the image she presented to the world was impeccable. She projected glamour, efficiency and capability. No one meeting Avery Scott could ever doubt that she would get the job done and that it would be done perfectly. She had an address book that would have made an ambitious socialite sob with envy but few knew the woman beneath the surface.

She'd shut him out. The closer he'd tried to get, the more she'd blocked him.

He almost laughed at the irony. He'd spent his life preventing women from getting too close. With Avery that tactic had proved unnecessary. *She* was the one who'd erected the barriers. And when he'd pushed up against those barriers too hard, she'd simply walked away.

They'd been lovers for a year, friends for longer, but

still there had been days when he'd felt he didn't know her. But there were some things he *did* know. Like the way a tiny dimple always appeared in the corner of her mouth when she smiled, and the fact that her mouth was addictive. Remembering that taste stirred up a response he'd thought he had under control.

The first time he'd met her he'd been attracted by her confidence and by the way she squeezed every drop of opportunity from life. He'd admired her drive, her success and her utter belief in herself. But the same qualities that had attracted him were the reasons they'd parted. Avery Scott was fiercely independent and terrified of anything she believed threatened that independence.

And he'd threatened it.

What they'd shared had threatened it. And so she'd ended it. Crushed what they had until there was nothing left but the pain.

People assumed that a man of his position had everything.

They had no idea how wrong they were.

Mal stood for a moment, tasting the unpalatable combination of regret and anger and at that moment she looked up and saw him.

He searched for some evidence that his unexpected appearance affected her, but there was nothing. Outwardly composed, she rose to her feet, elegant and in control and displaying the same unflappable calm she demonstrated even in a crisis. 'This is a surprise. How can I help you, Mal?' Cool. Professional. No hint that they'd once been as close as it was possible for two people to be, apart from the fact that she'd called him Mal.

His name had slipped from those glossy lips without thought and yet only a handful of close friends ever called him that. And Avery had once been in that hallowed circle. She knew his closest friends because she'd been one of them; one of the few people indifferent to his wealth or his status. One of the few people who'd treated him like a man and not like the next ruler of Zubran. For a while, when he'd been with her, he'd forgotten about duty and responsibility.

Mal thrust that thought aside along with the others. Those days were gone. Today's visit was all about duty and responsibility. He wasn't going to make this personal. He couldn't.

He was about to marry another woman.

'You didn't pick up your phone.' He dispensed with formal greetings or pleasantries, considering them unnecessary.

'I was in a meeting. You, a world leader who is generally considered an expert in the art of diplomacy, will surely understand that I couldn't interrupt a client.' She spoke in the same neutral tone he'd heard her use with difficult clients.

Somewhere deep inside him he felt his nerve endings spark and fire and he remembered that their verbal sparring matches had been their second favourite way of passing the time they spent together.

As for the first…

His libido roared to life and Mal turned to the other woman in the room, because privacy was essential for the conversation he was about to have. 'Leave us, please.'

Responding to that command without question, the woman rose. As the door closed behind her Avery turned on him, blue eyes ice-cold.

'You just can't help it, can you? You just can't help telling people what to do.'

'This is not a conversation I intend to conduct in public.'

'This is my office. My business. You are not in charge here. Whatever your reason for being here, nothing justifies you walking in without knocking and breaking up my meeting. I wouldn't do it to you. I don't expect you to do it to me.'

It was as if a high-voltage electrical current had suddenly been diverted through the room. It crackled, sizzled and threatened to leave them both singed, and it aggravated him as much as he knew it irritated her.

'Why wouldn't you take my calls?'

Two streaks of colour darkened her cheeks. 'You called at inconvenient moments.'

'And does ignoring your clients' phone calls generally work well for you? I'd always assumed that customer service is everything in your business.'

'You weren't calling about business.'

'And you weren't thinking about business when you refused to take my calls so let's stop pretending we don't know what's going on here.' Deeply unsettled by the strength of his own feelings, Mal strode to the huge glass windows that enveloped her office and reminded himself that his reason for being here had nothing to do with his past relationship with this woman. That was irrelevant. It *had* to be irrelevant. 'Nice views. You've done extraordinarily well for yourself. Your business is booming while others fold.'

'Why do you find it extraordinary? I work hard and I understand my market.'

Her reply made him smile but he kept that smile to himself. 'Less than five minutes together and already you're picking a fight.'

'You're the one who landed a helicopter on my roof and barged into my office. I would say you were the one picking the fight, Mal.'

For the first time in weeks he felt the energy flow through him. Not to anyone would he have admitted how good it felt to have someone speak without restraint. To argue with him. *To challenge—*

'I was merely congratulating you on the astonishing growth of your business in a difficult economic climate.'

'You could have done that in an email. I have absolutely no idea why you're here or why you've been phoning me every two minutes but I'm assuming you don't want to talk about guest lists or colour schemes.'

'I am not remotely interested in the details of the party. That is your job.'

'For once we're in agreement. And now I'd be grateful if you'd leave so that I can do that job.'

Sufficiently energized, he turned. 'No one but you would dare speak to me like that.'

'So fire me, Mal. Go on. Do it. Take your business elsewhere.' Those eyes locked on his and he wondered why she would be encouraging him to back out of what must be for her a prime piece of business. Under the perfectly applied make-up, she looked tired. His gaze slid to her hands and he saw her fiddling nervously with the pen she was holding.

Avery never fiddled. Avery was never nervous.

His attention caught, he watched her for a moment, trying to read her. 'I'm not firing you.'

'Then at least get to the point. Why are you here?'

'I'm here because at the moment the party cannot go ahead. Something crucial is missing.'

The mere suggestion that something might be less than perfect had her bristling defensively as she always did if anyone so much as questioned her competence. That beautifully shod foot tapped the floor. Those eyes narrowed as she mentally scrolled through the checklist she kept permanently updated in her head. 'I can assure you that nothing is "missing", Mal. I have been over the plans meticulously and checked every last detail personally. It will all be absolutely as planned.'

She had complete confidence in her own ability and that confidence was justified because Avery Scott never overlooked anything. Nothing escaped her. Her attention to detail drove her team mad. It had driven *him* mad, and yet at the same time he'd admired it because she'd built herself a successful business on the back of nothing but her own hard work. This woman had never freeloaded in her life. Nor had she ever asked anyone for anything. She was the first woman he'd met who wasn't interested in anything he had to offer.

For a moment he felt a pang of regret, but regret was a sentiment he couldn't afford and he moved on quickly.

'You misunderstand me. I'm sure that everything your company has planned is perfect, as ever.'

'So if that is the case, what can possibly be missing?'

Mal paused, hesitating because he was about to trust her with information that he hadn't entrusted to another living soul. Even now he was wondering whether coming here had been a mistake.

'What am I missing? The most important thing of all,' he drawled softly. 'I'm missing my bride.'

CHAPTER TWO

'YOUR *bride*?' The word clung to her dry mouth. Oh God, she was cracking up. The effort of holding it together was just too much. It was bad enough that he was here in person, but the fact that he was here to talk about his bride was a double blow. Did he have no tact? No sensitivity at all?

Shock cut through the sickness she felt at seeing him. She needed to think, but that was impossible with him dominating her office in that sleek dark suit that emphasised the width of those shoulders and the muscular strength of his powerful frame. It bothered her that she noticed his body. It bothered her even more to feel the answering response in her own. This office was her personal space. Having it invaded by him felt difficult and she hated the fact that it felt difficult because she so badly wanted to feel nothing. She was used to being in control of herself at all times. Wanted it most of all at *this* time.

But as that control slipped from her, she felt a buzz of panic. Over the past year she'd turned off news coverage about economic and political stability in his country. Even though her company was responsible for the evening party to follow his wedding, she'd averted her eyes from stories about that event. If she didn't need to read it, she didn't read it. When their paths crossed at events she was organizing or attending as a guest, she restricted their contact to a brief nod across a crowded room even though the only man in the room she ever saw was him. She'd avoided it all in an attempt to regain control of her life and her feelings. Everything she did, she did to protect herself. Mal had hurt her. And he'd hurt her so badly that seeing him now brought her right back to the edge.

What frightened her most wasn't the sense of power and authority that could subdue a room full of people, nor was it his spectacular looks, even though the lethal combination of dark masculinity and perfect musculature was sufficient to make happily married women contemplate infidelity. No, what frightened her—*what made her truly vulnerable*—was the sensual gleam in those dangerous black eyes.

He was the most sexual man she'd ever met. Or maybe it was just their history that made her think that about him.

The look he gave her was reserved for her and her alone. It was a look that blatantly acknowledged a past she would rather have forgotten. It made every interaction deeply personal and the last thing she wanted was personal. She wanted to forget every intimacy they'd ever shared.

He was marrying another woman.

Remembering that, she kept her tone neutral and refused to let herself respond to that velvety dark gaze that threatened to strip away every defence she'd constructed between them. This wasn't about her. It was about his bride.

'Kalila is missing?' Despite her own tangled emotions and natural instinct for self-preservation, she felt a rush of concern. She'd met Kalila on a few occasions and had found her friendly, if rather shy. The girl had seemed more than a little overwhelmed by the Prince even though they'd reportedly known one another for years. 'Are you saying she's been kidnapped or something?'

'No, not kidnapped.'

'But if she's missing, how can you be so sure she hasn't

been kidnapped? I mean, she is a princess. I suppose there are people who—'

'A note was delivered to me.'

'A note?' Her brain wasn't working properly. All she could think about was him. 'But—'

'Not a ransom note. A note from her.'

'I don't understand.' It was a struggle to concentrate. Looking at him sent images chasing into her head. Images that usually only haunted her when she slept.

'She has run away—' The words were offered up with obvious reluctance and Avery stared at him in silence. And that silence stretched so long that in the end he broke it with an impatient gesture. 'Her reasons are irrelevant.'

'Irrelevant?' She shook her head to clear it of all the thoughts she shouldn't be having. What would have driven the shy, compliant Kalila to do something so radical? 'How can her reasons possibly be irrelevant? How can you dismiss her views like that?'

'I'm not dismissing her views. But what matters is not the reasons she left, but getting her back.'

'And you don't think the two of those things might be linked? Why did she leave? For someone like Kalila to do something so dramatic, she must have had a really good reason.'

'She doesn't want this marriage.' He spoke through his teeth and Avery wondered if the tension she heard in his tone reflected his irritation at the disruption of his plans or his sentiments towards his bride-to-be.

Mal was a man who was relentlessly sure of himself, a skilled negotiator, composed and in control and she knew from personal experience that he didn't react well to anything that disrupted his plans.

'Oh dear.' It was a pathetic commentary on the situation but the best she could come up with. 'That *is* inconvenient. Hard to get married without a bride, I do see that.'

'It is far more than "inconvenient". This wedding *must* go ahead.'

'Because it is what her father wants?'

'Because it is what *I* want. I need to reassure her that our marriage can work. I need her to know I am nothing like her father. I can protect her.'

Avery stared at him numbly.

Had he ever been this protective of her? No. Of course not. And she wouldn't have wanted him to be. She didn't *need* protecting, did she? She never had. What hurt was the fact that he could move from one woman to another with such ease. 'So you're about to leap onto horseback wielding your sword to protect her. Good. That's…good. I'm sure she'll appreciate the gesture.' All this time she'd been telling herself that this marriage was no more than a political union. That he didn't have feelings for Kalila.

Clearly she'd been wrong about that, too.

He had *strong* feelings. Why else would he be so determined to go through with this?

Her throat felt thick. There was a burning sensation behind her eyes.

Fortunately he didn't notice. 'She is extremely vulnerable. Not that I'd expect you to understand that. You don't do "vulnerable", do you?'

He had no idea. 'I understand that you want to slay her dragons.'

'Whereas you would rather a man gave you a dragon so that you could slay it yourself.'

'I'm an animal lover. If you'd bought me a dragon I would have kept it as a pet.'

Once, an exchange like that would have ended in laughter. He would have challenged her. She would have challenged him right back and eventually the clash would have led where it always led—to the bedroom, or any other place that could afford them the privacy they craved.

'I simply think it would be wiser if she learned to protect herself.'

'Not every woman is like you.' There was a dark bitterness in his tone that stung wounds still not healed. She'd started to despair they ever would be.

Her stress levels soared skyward. Her jaw ached from clenching her teeth. Her insides were churning and suddenly she wished she hadn't drunk the coffee on an empty stomach. 'I do see your problem. It's hard to get married without a bride. However, while I sympathise with your dilemma and applaud your macho protective streak, which I'm sure your bride will find extremely touching, I really don't understand my role in this. I carry spares of most things, but not brides I'm afraid.'

'Kalila liked you. She admired you. She considered you her friend. Or as close to a friend as someone with her life could ever have.' His wide shoulders shifted slightly as if he were trying to ease tension and she realised that he was every bit as stressed as she was. There was a glint in those eyes, a simmering tension in that powerful frame that told her he was feeling what she was feeling. 'I'm asking for your help.'

'*My* help?' She wondered why he made her feel vulnerable. She was tall, but his height and build overpowered her. 'I don't understand how I can possibly help.' Looking at him now, she wondered how they'd ever sustained their relationship for so long. He was so autocratic. Very much the Crown Prince, a man of breathtaking power and influence. There was no sign of the man who had laughed with her and enjoyed philosophical arguments long into the night. *This* man was austere and, yes, intimidating.

Those eyes looked straight through to her mind, seeing things she didn't want him to see. He'd once told her that he could judge a person's reaction more accurately from what they did than what they said. It was a skill that had stood him in good stead in handling diplomatic tensions between neighbouring countries.

Remembering that, she stood still and did nothing. She didn't allow her gaze to slide from his. If her body language wasn't silent, then at least it was muted. 'I cannot imagine what help I can possibly offer. I organize parties. I have it on good authority that I lead a life of unimpeded frivolity.'

The glance he sent her told her that he remembered that bitter exchange as well as she did. Her business had been just one more point of contention between them.

'You are a resourceful and independent woman and you knew her. She talked to you—' he ignored her reference to their past '—I wondered if you had any idea where she might have gone. Think back to your conversations. Did she ever say anything that might be of use? Anything at all.'

She'd been trying to forget those conversations. She'd been trying to forget Kalila altogether because whenever she imagined her, she imagined her entwined with Mal and the image was so painful to view she wanted to close her eyes and scream.

Feeling her hands start to shake again, Avery clasped them behind her back. 'I honestly don't—'

'Come on, Avery, *think*! What did you talk about?' His voice was harsh. 'Several times you talked to her at parties. You helped her choose a dress when she hosted that charity dinner. You put her in touch with her wedding dress designer. She idolized you. You were her role model. She longed to be like you.'

'Really?' A small laugh escaped. Afraid that she sounded

hysterical, she clamped her mouth shut. 'Well, that's ironic. I'm sure you talked her out of that fast enough.'

His only response to that oblique reference to their shared past was a slight tightening of his beautiful mouth. 'Did she say anything?'

'No.' *Leave, why don't you? Just leave,* she thought. But of course he didn't because the Prince didn't leave until he had what he wanted. 'I honestly don't know where she would have gone.' And worry slowly uncurled itself inside her because Kalila *was* vulnerable and Avery didn't like to think of any woman being vulnerable. As soon as Mal left, she'd call her. Not that there were any guarantees that she'd pick up the phone but at least she would have tried.

'Did she mention a particular place to you?' Those ebony eyes locked on hers, his intention no doubt to increase the impact of his words. Instead he succeeded only in increasing the intimacy and the chemistry between them. His response to that was to frown. Hers was to back away, hit by such a powerful need to touch him that retreat seemed like the only option. And of course he noticed that step backwards, because he was a man who noticed everything.

The tension snapped tight between them. Heat poured through her body and into her pelvis and still he looked at her and she looked right back at him because to look away was something her pride wouldn't allow. Or maybe it was just because she couldn't. The look connected them in a way far deeper than any verbal exchange and Avery felt her stomach plunge.

'You're the one with a high-tech security team just a phone call away.' Somehow her voice sounded normal. 'Can't they track her down?'

'Not so far. We think she might have adopted a disguise, but I can't question people without raising suspicions and I want to solve this as discreetly as possible.'

'Have you talked to her friends?'

'She wasn't allowed friends. She was raised in a very protected environment.'

Avery remembered her saying as much when they'd spoken. Remembered thinking how odd it must be to live like that, a prisoner of luxury, locked away from reality.

'You're the one marrying her. You should be the one who knows where she is.'

'We've spent very little time together.' The admission was dragged from him with obvious reluctance and he paced over to the window, leaving her only with a view of his back. 'I admit that was a failing on my part. I made assumptions.'

'You always do. You always know what's best for everyone.'

The tension in his shoulders increased but he chose not to respond to that. 'That is not important right now. What is important is finding her. If this marriage does not go ahead there will be serious diplomatic consequences.'

'Diplomatic consequences?' Avery rolled her eyes in exasperation at his priorities. 'No wonder Kalila left—it's not very romantic, is it?'

'I'm surprised you're even able to recognise a romantic.' He stood like a conqueror, powerful legs spread apart as he stared down at the view.

'Why? Because I'm not romantic myself? We're not talking about me.' Reflecting on the fact that men could be truly clueless when it came to women, she tried to control her emotions. 'She really gave you no clue that she felt this way? The two of you have known each other for years.'

'We've barely spoken five words to each other.'

Avery hid her surprise. 'Oh.' *So if he didn't love Kalila, why had he been in such a hurry to marry her?* Only one explanation presented itself. They'd broken up. He was angry. He'd done it to hurt her.

'On the few occasions she spoke to me, she usually just agreed with whatever I was saying.'

Numb, Avery thought about all the lively debates they'd shared on every topic from economics to human rights and wondered how a man like Mal could be happy with a wife whose sole purpose in life was to agree with him.

He'd be bored rigid.

And it would serve him right if he were consigned to a life of misery for taking this enormous step just to score points against her.

'If she's that obedient maybe you should have just ordered her to "sit" and "stay".'

'This is *not* the time for sarcasm. I came to see if you could shed any light on her whereabouts.'

'I can't. And truly I cannot imagine why you would ask me.' And now she was just desperate for him to leave, not just because of the way he made her feel but because she wanted to call Kalila and make a few enquiries of her own.

It wasn't right that Kalila should be used as a pawn in their fight.

'You and I were friends once—' He turned his head to look at her and just for a moment she saw the past in his eyes. 'Good friends.'

What he'd introduced into the room was more frightening than any dragon. 'Mal—'

'I'm asking you as a friend. There are few enough people I can trust in my life but, despite everything, I do trust you. Whatever happened between us, I still trust you and I realise that this situation is potentially awkward—' His dark gaze fastened on her like some sort of high-tech imaging device designed to penetrate flesh and bone in the search for truth. 'If you still had feelings for me I would never have involved you. You ended our relationship so I assumed that wasn't the case. If I was wrong about that then tell me now.'

Tell him what? That she dreamed about him every night? That she found it hard to focus and that it took her twice as long to accomplish simple tasks because she was preoccupied? That in the months following their break-up she'd barely recognised the woman she'd become?

Even now, she sometimes looked in the mirror and saw a stranger staring back at her.

Avery's mouth was dry. Her heart was bumping against her chest so hard she was surprised he couldn't see it. *'If you still had feelings for me—'* No mention of *his* feelings. Which shouldn't have surprised her and certainly shouldn't have hurt. If he'd had feelings for her he wouldn't have been able to move with such ease from one woman to another.

'I don't have feelings.' She adopted the chilly tone she used when men tried to get too close to her at functions. 'My inability to help you has nothing to do with our history, but the fact that I have no useful information.'

'What did you talk about when you were together?'

'I can't remember—' she didn't *want* to remember because talking to his bride had been like sticking knives into herself '—shoes, dresses and education for women. She never talked about running away.' Or had she? The ghost of a memory flitted into her head. Avery gave a tiny frown and Mal spotted the change in her instantly, pouncing like a lion on a gazelle.

'What?'

'Nothing.' She shook her head. 'I—'

'"Nothing" is all I have to go on right now.'

'Is there a chance she might have gone into the desert?'

Mal's expression changed. His eyes were shuttered. 'Definitely not. Kalila hates the desert.'

'I know.' And she'd always thought it really odd that a girl raised in that landscape could loathe it. Even more strange that she'd agreed to marry a man whose love for the desert was widely known. 'She told me how much it scared her—' She broke off, an uncomfortable memory pricking her conscience.

His eyes narrowed as he registered the guilt in her face. 'And what advice did you offer on that topic?'

Avery felt her cheeks heat. 'We might have had a conversation about facing our fears,' she muttered. 'Just a short one.'

His mouth tightened ominously. 'And?'

'And nothing. I just said that the best way to get over being afraid of something is to just do it, which actually is very sound advice, but *obviously* that comment wasn't directed specifically at her.' But what if she'd taken it that way? Avery shifted uncomfortably, her guilt trebling as she watched the colour drain from his handsome face.

'You told her that she should go into the desert alone?'

'No, of course not!' But Avery felt a stab of panic as she realised how her words could have been interpreted. 'I just suggested that sometimes it's empowering to do something that scares you. That you learn you can cope with it and you come out stronger.'

'Or you come out dead. Do you realise how dangerous the desert is for someone with no experience or expertise in desert survival?'

'Yes! And I don't know why you're blaming me!' Her voice rose. 'I did *not* tell her to go into the desert alone.'

'Then let's hope that isn't what she's done. She would last five minutes.' Anxiety stamped into his features, Mal pulled out his phone and made a call, talking rapidly to his security team while Avery stood there, an agonized witness to his obvious worry and feeling hideously responsible for the part she'd possibly played.

What if Kalila really had taken her literally and gone into the desert alone?

Surely she wouldn't have done anything so foolish. *Would she?*

Her brain argued it back and forth and eventually she pressed her fingers to her forehead as if by doing so she might be able to shut down her thoughts. 'Look, maybe I can—'

'You've done enough. Thank you for your help. You've told me all I need to know.' He was chillingly formal. There was a hardness to him that she didn't remember ever seeing before. He was tough, yes, and she knew that most people found him intimidating, but she never had. And he hadn't found her intimidating either. Unlike many men, he hadn't been daunted by her success and that had been so refreshing.

'This is *not* my fault.' But her voice lacked conviction because deep down she was afraid that it was at least partially her fault. Had she unwittingly put the idea in Kalila's head? 'And if that is what she's done, then maybe it isn't such a bad thing. Maybe this will build her confidence in herself. I think it was very brave of her to go into the desert if that is what she's done…' Her voice tailed off as he turned on her savagely.

'*Brave?*' Contempt dripped from him. 'Will you think she's "brave" when she's been bitten by a scorpion? Caught in a sandstorm? Drowned in a flash flood?'

Guilt ignited her own temper. 'Maybe she'll surprise you. And maybe the experience will be the making of her. Maybe it will give her the courage to stand up for herself and tell you what she wants. And whether it does or doesn't, you should ask yourself why she finds the prospect of those things less scary than marriage. She's run into the desert to get away from you, Mal!'

The truth earned her a fierce look. 'You are assuming that her disappearance is some sort of statement about our relationship.'

'Well, that's how it looks from where I'm standing.'

'She agreed to this. She wanted this marriage.'

'How would you know? Did you even ask her? Or did you "assume" like you always assume. Maybe she didn't want this marriage and she was afraid to tell you.' Avery knew she should stop talking. Stop now, before something was said that couldn't be unsaid, but she couldn't help herself. 'Maybe marriage was the last thing she wanted.'

'Not every woman sees marriage as captivity to be avoided at all costs.' His eyes clashed with hers and her heart started to race because suddenly they weren't talking about Kalila.

They were sparring, as they'd always sparred. The only difference was that this encounter wasn't going to end with their mouths and bodies locked together. And he was clearly thinking along the same lines because a tiny frown appeared between those bold black eyebrows and his eyes darkened dangerously.

The air was stifling.

Avery wondered how the conversation had shifted from safe territory to unsafe territory. Had that been her fault or his?

'We were talking about Kalila.' She snapped the words and then hated herself for appearing anything other than calm in his presence.

'Yes. Kalila.' His voice was thick and it was clear he wasn't faring any better than she was with the direction the conversation had taken.

'All I'm saying is that maybe she expressed her opinion in the only way she was able. She voted with her feet. I don't know anything about the politics of this situation, nor do I want to, but you asked me what I thought and—'

'No, I didn't. I already know your position on marriage so I would never ask. Our opinions on that subject are in direct opposition, as we both know.'

Why did he keep bringing the subject back to her when it should have been his bride-to-be that they were discussing?

'As you rightly point out, I am unlikely to have the faintest clue what Kalila is feeling. But it's obvious she's panicking about the wedding.' And now perhaps she was lying in the desert, gasping with thirst or worse… Perhaps she was already unconscious, her frail body being pecked by giant birds.

Crap.

'What is obvious to me is that she has indeed followed your advice and gone into the desert. It would explain why we can find no trace of her in the city.' Anger shone in his eyes. 'I suppose it's too much to ask to expect you to know exactly where she went? Was there a particular place that you recommended as perfect for her to "face her fears"?'

Avery squirmed. 'No! But maybe I could—'

'You've already done more than enough.' He strode towards the door. 'Thank you for your time. I know how precious it is, so feel free to bill me.'

So that was it. He was leaving.

The pressure in her throat increased. 'Mal—'

'I have to go. I do not want to leave this innocent girl out there at the mercy of the desert and the capricious whims of the man who she is unfortunate enough to have as a father. She is extremely vulnerable.'

Avery felt something twist inside her. She felt an irrational spurt of jealousy for the woman who had dragged such tender feelings out of a man known for his lack of sentimentality. Mal was tough. A soldier and a skilled diplomat, used to dealing with the toughest of adversaries. She'd never seen him reveal any soft, sensitive feelings before. The fact that he was doing so now for another woman made her insides ache.

Whatever his reasons for marrying Kalila, it seemed he *did* care for her.

Any tension between them had been burned away by that exchange and now he was chillingly detached. 'I will let you know if the wedding party is likely to proceed. In the meantime you can put your arrangements on hold and invoice me for any costs incurred to date.'

'For goodness' sake, stop talking about money! I don't care about the money. I'm worried about Kalila, too. Wait!'

'I have a desert to search.'

'Then I'll search it with you.' The words came tumbling out of her mouth and she didn't know which one of them was the more surprised. He turned to face her, incredulity lighting his eyes.

'I beg your pardon?'

Avery took a step backwards but the words were out there now and they couldn't be withdrawn. She couldn't believe she'd actually said it. A moment ago she hadn't been able to wait for him to leave and now she was suggesting travelling into the desert with him? What the hell was she doing? When their relationship had crashed she'd almost lost everything. Everything she'd worked so hard to build. What they'd shared had been so intense, so powerful, and here she was volunteering to risk exposing those raw tender feelings again, and all so that she could help him marry another woman.

Avery wanted to pull the words back but her conscience

wouldn't let her. 'If Kalila had thought she could talk to you, then she would have talked to you. If you do find her—'

'*When* I find her—' His eyes promised all sorts of dire punishments if that didn't happen and Avery swallowed.

'Of course, that's what I meant. *When* you find her, you'll need to have a proper conversation, but what if she won't talk to you? She's never managed to talk to you before, has she? Why would she talk to you now? She's more likely to talk to me.'

There was a long, throbbing silence.

'Let me get this straight—' dark lashes shielded the expression in those ebony eyes '—you're offering to help find my bride and then talk her into marrying me?'

'Absolutely.' Avery forced the words out and he stared at her for a long moment as if he were trying to peel away the layers and see beneath the façade she presented to the world. 'Why not?'

Her question was greeted by prolonged silence and then he straightened his shoulders. 'I thought maybe—' his voice was rough '—it might be difficult for you to see me marrying another woman.'

'Difficult?' She hoped her laugh sounded more convincing to him than it did to her. 'Why would you think that? Our relationship is in the past, Mal. No one is more enthusiastic to see you married than I am. How else am I going to organize an after-wedding-party and bill you for shedloads of money? Let's get this done.'

CHAPTER THREE

'You said *what*? OK, now I know for sure you're mad. You're going into the desert to find a wimpy princess who doesn't have the courage to speak her own mind so that she can marry the man you were in love with?' Jenny lay sprawled on the bed in Avery's apartment, watching as her friend packed. 'It's like something out of a really bad soap opera. Scratch that—no one could make this stuff up. It is going to end in tears. And those are going to be *your* tears, by the way.'

'I've never cried over a man in my life. And stop saying I was in love with him.' A skilled packer, Avery rolled a couple of shirts to prevent them creasing. 'And Kalila isn't wimpy. It's not her fault if she's been bullied into submission all her life by her father. I feel sorry for her. Better not to have a father around than have a bad one.'

'Let's leave your father issues out of this. There's enough going on without that.'

'I do not have father issues.'

Jenny rearranged the pillows and cushions on the bed and slumped against them. 'What I don't understand is why the Prince would even ask you to do this. That must have taken some nerve.'

'He didn't ask. I offered. Without a bride he can't get married and I want him married.'

'You *want* him married?'

'Of course.' Avery added two pairs of trousers to her packing. Once he was married there would be no going back. If nothing else could kill her feelings for Mal, then surely marriage would. It would bring the finality she'd been looking for. 'And I want the party to go ahead. It's bad for business if a party is cancelled.'

'So you're doing this for the business?'

'I'm doing it because I'm worried about Kalila. You should have seen the way he looked at me when I told him what I'd said to her. As if I'd pushed her into the lion's cage and locked the door from the outside. I like her.'

'Really? She sounds like a wimp to me.'

'I think she's a victim of her circumstances. She's sweet. And yes, I feel responsible.' Avery sorted through her make-up, picking out the bare minimum she needed in order to not look like a train wreck. 'And guilty. That is the last time I ever tell anyone to face their fears.'

Jenny picked up a lipgloss and tried it on the back of her hand. 'You're not responsible for the fact she clearly has appalling judgement and did something rash and stupid. Nice colour, by the way.'

'Maybe I am responsible.' Avery rescued the lipgloss and added it to her bag. 'I was the one who put the idea in her head. Without me, she wouldn't even have thought of doing something so radical.' She packed carefully, referring to the list on her phone, knowing that the right clothing might be all that stood between her and an unpleasant experience in the desert. She picked items designed to cover her, not just because of concessions towards modesty or even protection against the sun, but because she wanted to do nothing that might be remotely described as provocative. The last thing she needed was Mal thinking she was trying to attract his attention.

'This is ridiculous. You're running a business, Avery. You don't have time to gallivant off after some woman you barely know with a guy you used to date. You should have—what are those—?' Jenny stared in alarm as Avery packed her sturdy hiking boots.

'"Those" are going to save me from snake bites and scorpion stings.'

Jenny recoiled. 'OK, forget my last sentence. No wonder the Princess ran away. She isn't wimpy, she's sensible. She's thinking long-term. Better a brief stint in the desert now than a lifetime of the place. If I had to wear boots like that I wouldn't marry the Prince either. It was meant to be a glass slipper, honey, not a hiking boot.'

'The desert is beautiful. Wild and stunning.'

'This from a woman who never likes to be more than ten minutes from a spa?'

'Actually I did stay in a spa while I was there, but I also stayed in a Bedouin camp and I enjoyed that as much. It's a really romantic place.'

'You're not romantic.' Jenny shook her head slowly. 'You're in trouble; you know that, don't you?'

Yes, she knew that. 'I'm not in trouble. I know what I'm doing. I'm in control.'

Jenny flopped back against the cushions. 'So I guess this means I'll have to call the Senator myself and break the news about the swans and the balloons.'

'Yes. Just speak with authority. And if there are problems you can call me. I'll have my phone. What I might not have is a signal. But Mal will have a satellite phone so I can use that to call you. You're not to tell anyone where we are. We're going to rescue her and then make up some story to cover her absence.'

'What sort of story?'

'I don't know. The spa idea is a good one. Maybe she

and I went into the desert for a girly break or something.
I just need you to be vague. If anyone asks, tell them I'm
with a friend. I'll be gone two days. Three at the most.'
Avery caught Jenny's expression. 'What? Why are you
looking at me like that?'

'You're assuming she's going to want to come back with
you, marry Mal and live happily ever after. What if it
doesn't happen like that?'

'It will.'

'She ran away from him.'

'They just need to start communicating with each other.
It will be fine.' *She was going to make sure it was fine.*

'I hope you're right.' Jenny handed her a bottle of sunscreen that had fallen out of her bag. 'In the meantime, you
don't even know where to start looking.'

'We've got a few ideas. I've already spoken to Kalila's
sister. She thinks she's probably hiding out in a desert com-
munity she was sent to when she was a teenager so we're
going to start there.'

'Like a summer camp?'

'That sort of thing.' Avery found her passport and
dropped it into her bag. 'It's a find-yourself, Zen type of
place.'

'Camp with scorpions. Thank goodness my parents
didn't send me to that one.' Jenny shuddered but Avery
didn't smile because she knew her problem wasn't going
to be the desert wildlife or even the inhospitable terrain.

It was Mal. Or, more specifically, her feelings about
Mal.

'The scorpions aren't a problem as long as you remember to shake your boots out in the morning before you put
them on and you're careful about moving rocks and things.'

Jenny curled her legs under her. 'You are the woman

who knows everything there is to know about throwing a good party. When did you learn about scorpions?'

'I spent time in the desert with Mal.' And she didn't want to think about that now. Didn't dare think about it, but of course having heard that comment Jenny wasn't about to let it go.

'He's the Crown Prince. I assumed that when he went into the desert he had jewel-encrusted tents and hundreds of people to wait on him. Surely scorpions aren't allowed in the royal presence?'

'His father sent him to spend a year with a desert tribe to understand how they lived. And he spent a couple of years in the Zubrani military after Cambridge. He knows the desert, although this is different because we're travelling into Arhmor, which is where his princess comes from. Which hat?' Avery held two of them up and when Jenny pointed she dropped it into her bag. 'Apparently we're pretending to be tourists.'

'Won't he be recognised? For that matter, won't *you* be recognised? With your blonde hair and your blue eyes, you're going to stand out like a pair of red shoes at a white wedding.'

'That's why I'm packing the hat.' Avery added a silk wrap to her packing. 'And anyway, no one will expect to see the Crown Prince of Zubran slumming it in a four-by-four, and because they don't expect to see him, they won't see him. But you make a good point. I don't think travelling in disguise is his thing. Can you grab me a baseball hat with "I love London" on it or something?'

Jenny shuddered. 'If I have to. But are you absolutely sure you're fine with travelling alone through the desert with a man you were once in love with?'

'I wasn't in love with him. I've told you that a thousand times.'

'Maybe after another thousand times I might actually believe you.' Jenny slid off the bed. 'I'm just worried this is going to be so hard for you.'

'It's not. It's going to cure me.' Avery snapped her case shut. 'Five minutes alone with Mal in the desert and he'll be driving me mad. I'll be doing everything I can to make sure he marries someone else. In fact I'll probably push her up the aisle myself.'

She was driving him mad.

Five minutes alone in her company and already Mal was asking himself how they'd ever survived a year together. No other woman had this effect on him. Certainly not the woman he was supposed to be marrying. His mouth tightened as he contemplated Kalila's obvious change of heart. Could he really blame her for running? They had no relationship and never had. He hadn't lied when he'd told Avery they'd barely spoken. What *had* been a lie was the implication that their lack of communication had been driven by Kalila's strict upbringing. In fact even when the opportunity had arisen, they'd had nothing to say to each other.

The marriage was about duty, nothing more. The deal was clearly as distasteful to Kalila as it was to him, but he'd made his choice and he'd thought she had too. And if there had been a moment in his life when he'd thought that duty and desire just might coincide, then that was in the past.

Except that the 'past' was hoisting a bag off her shoulder and glaring at him as if he were personally responsible for global warming and the economic crisis.

He was a fool to have allowed her to come. *To have put himself in this position.*

'I'll drive.' She slung her bag into the back of the four-by-four, slim and elegant in linen trousers and a long-sleeved shirt that shielded her slender arms from the sun.

That shiny blond fall of hair was restrained in a tight plait that fell between her narrow shoulder blades.

Mal dragged his eyes from the lean lines of her body and focused on her face. As always, her skin was flawless and her make-up perfect. There were no signs that she was finding the situation stressful. And why would she? She'd ended their relationship, hadn't she? And since that day—*that day now forged in his memory*—she'd shown no regrets about that decision.

'I'm driving.' He wanted to give himself something to focus on other than her. 'It will attract less attention.'

'The driver attracts more attention than the passenger. I will drive.'

'Are we going to argue every point?'

'That's up to you.' Her blue eyes were cool. 'If you're a tourist then you need to look like a tourist. Good job I brought you a gift from London.' She tossed a baseball hat at him and he caught it and read the words on the front.

'"*I love London*"?'

'I tried to get a matching T-shirt but no luck. They only had small or medium. At least you look slightly closer to "tourist" than you did five minutes ago.' Her eyes skimmed his shoulders. It was such a brief look that to an outsider it wouldn't have seemed significant but he was looking for other signs and this time he found them. The slight change in her breathing. The way she was careful to step away from him. 'Now all you have to do is stop ordering me around.'

'I have never ordered you around. You have always done exactly as you wanted to do.' Because he was still watching, he saw her expression flicker.

For a moment he thought she was going to say something personal. Possibly even admit that travelling alone together like this was far more difficult than she'd imagined it would be. But then she gave a careless smile.

'Good. So in that case you won't mind if I drive.' Breaking the connection, she opened the driver's door and was about to jump inside when he caught her arm and pulled her back to him. The contact was minimal but that was all it took, the attraction so deep, so fierce that he released her instantly. But it was too late because his body had already recognised her. This close, her perfume seeped into his senses and the scent of it was so evocative it acted like a brake to his thinking. He couldn't remember what he'd been about to say. He couldn't think about anything except how much he wanted her.

Her mouth was so close to his that he could feel the tiny shallow breaths that were her attempts to draw air into her lungs. He knew that mouth. *He wanted that mouth.*

Her eyes lifted to his and for one unguarded moment he saw something there he'd never seen before. Not pain. It was so much more than pain. Misery? Heartbreak? *Fear?* Even as he was struggling to name what he saw, it was gone—as if someone had closed a blind on a window, leaving him wondering if he'd imagined that brief glimpse into someone's strictly guarded privacy.

She was the one who looked away first. 'Fine, you drive if it bothers you so much.' There were many shades of emotion in her voice, but not the one he was looking for. He heard bored. He heard amused. He didn't hear heartbreak or pain and he assumed he'd conjured that from his own brain.

'Avery—'

Ignoring him, she strode round to the passenger side and dragged open the door. 'If you need to reinforce your masculinity behind the wheel, you go right ahead. Maybe you can spear us an antelope for lunch, or strangle us a rattlesnake with your bare hands. Whisk us up a tasty scorpion soup?' She sprang inside, lithe and athletic, the plait of her hair swinging across her back like a shiny golden rope. 'But drive at a decent pace, will you? Nothing makes me madder than tentative male drivers and you don't want to be trapped with me when I'm mad.'

Mal ground his teeth.

He didn't want to be trapped with her at all. It was already driving him mad.

Only the knowledge that she'd be useful once they found Kalila prevented him from making the decision to leave her behind.

He slid into the driver's seat. 'We will check the desert camp first. We should arrive there tomorrow morning.'

If she was unsettled at the thought of a night in the desert with him then she didn't let it show. 'You could just fly there in your helicopter.'

'Which would alert everyone to the fact that my bride has run away.' He snapped on his seat belt and eased the vehicle onto the dusty road. 'For obvious reasons I'm trying to avoid that. I'm trying to protect Kalila. If possible, I don't want her father to find out. Since my helicopter is emblazoned with the colours of the Royal Flight, using it would hardly help me stay under the radar.'

'Yes, it's not great publicity, I can see that. *The Prince and his Runaway Bride* isn't the best headline. Your PR team are going to have fun spinning that one.' As the vehicle hit a bump she gripped her seat. 'Any time you want me to drive, just let me know.'

'We have barely been moving for five minutes. You are a terrible passenger.'

'I like to be the one in control. If I'm going to die, I want to choose when and where. And generally, who with, but beggars can't be choosers.'

His mouth twitched. 'I'm an exceptionally good driver.'

'To be exceptionally good at something requires practice and you were virtually born in a chauffeur-driven armoured limousine.'

'I frequently drive myself unless I have work to do. I fly myself, too. And you know it.' He gave her a sideways glance and met her glare.

'Keep your eyes on the road. You need to be in one piece when you meet up with your little virgin princess.'

'As a matter of interest, is your objection to the fact she is a virgin or a princess?'

'I don't have any objections. It was just a descriptive phrase.'

'Interesting choice of words. You don't like Kalila?'

'I like her very much.' She leaned forward and fished in her bag for a pair of sunglasses. She slid them on, protecting her eyes from the harsh glare of the desert sun. 'I happen to think she's perfect for you.'

'Meaning?'

'She won't ever disagree with you. Whatever you do or say, you'll always be the one in charge and sweet Kalila will admire you and never question whether you're right or not because it wouldn't enter her head that you wouldn't be.'

'That could be because I *am* right.' He saw the smile curve her soft lips and felt a rush of irritation. 'Kalila is a sweet-natured, compliant young woman.'

'As I said—' she adjusted her glasses with a perfectly manicured finger '—perfect for you. Oh look! Are those gazelle?'

Dragging his eyes from those slim fingers, he followed the direction of her gaze and watched as a small herd of slender gazelle sprinted away. From this distance they appeared to be floating on the sand. 'Yes. You think I am afraid to be challenged?'

'You hate to be challenged, Mal. And it happens so rarely you're unlikely to have the opportunity to get used to it. Which is why you always assume you're right. Isn't it unusual to see herds of gazelle here? What type are they?' She reached into her bag for her phone so that she could take a photograph. 'They're *gorgeous*. So graceful.'

'They are sand gazelle—the word gazelle comes from the Arabic *ḡazāl*. We support numerous conservation projects. Protecting wildlife and preserving their natural habitat is important to us. Killing and capture of all wildlife is illegal in Zubran. And you should stop changing the subject.'

'I love the colour of their coats. So pale.'

'Typical of you to comment on their appearance.' His gaze flickered briefly to the plait of blonde hair that gleamed like gold in the sunlight. 'The sand gazelle has adapted for life in the desert. The coat reflects the sun's rays instead of absorbing them and of course it provides camouflage. And, by the way, I have no objection at all to being challenged.' He knew she was trying to rile him and wondered why she would feel the need when the atmosphere in the car was already heavy with tension. 'My wife will be my equal.'

Her laughter was spontaneous and genuine and she was still laughing as she slipped her phone back into her bag. 'Sorry, but you have to admit that's funny.'

'*What* is funny?'

'You thinking that your wife will be your equal. In which universe, Mal?'

It was a struggle to hang onto his temper. 'She *will* be my equal.'

'As long as she agrees with you.' Laughter gone, she was cool and suddenly he wanted to shake that cool.

'So the thought of me marrying her doesn't upset you?'

'Why would I be upset?' The sunglasses were back on her nose, obscuring her expression. 'You are free to marry whomever you choose. It's none of my business, although I'm wishing now I'd made it my business. I should have called Kalila and given her the chance for girl talk. Poor thing.'

'Poor thing? You and I were together for over a year.'

'It felt much, much longer, don't you think? And now we're not together, which is a big relief for both of us. If you're asking me if news of your wedding was a shock, then the answer is no. I always knew you'd get married. You're the marrying kind, Mal.' Her answer was just a little too swift. A little too glib.

'And what is "the marrying kind"?'

'Someone who wants to get married, obviously. People get married for different reasons. Sometimes it's because they need financial security. Sometimes it's because they're too maladjusted to live by themselves—' she suppressed a yawn '—increasingly it's because they see divorce as a lucrative option. In your case it's because you have a sense of responsibility towards your father and your country. You feel a duty to produce children and for that you need a wife because you wouldn't contemplate any other alternative.'

Mal had forgotten just how cynical she was about marriage.

He assumed her extreme reaction was somehow linked with her own background but, apart from telling him her mother had raised her alone, she'd given him no details. They'd spent their time in the present, never revisiting the past.

Would things have been different, he wondered, if he'd questioned her more? Would it have helped if he'd gained more insight into the workings of her mind?

'You think those are the only reasons for marriage?' He drove fast, speeding along one of the wide roads that crossed the desert, wishing they'd never started this conversation. Truthfully, he didn't want to talk about his impending marriage. He didn't want to *think* about it until the moment came to make his vows. He'd delayed for as long as he could and now it was oppressively close, reality pressing in on him like dark clouds.

It was true that he'd proposed marriage to Kalila within weeks of his relationship with Avery breaking down, but there were reasons for that. Reasons he hadn't shared with her and didn't intend to share with her.

What was the point?

Her phone rang and she took the call. Already this morning she'd been on the phone to the office at least four times, addressing problems.

'Doves?' Mal failed to keep the sarcasm out of his voice as she ended yet another call. 'You really do deal with the big issues, don't you?'

'If you're implying that my business has no value then I feel obliged to point out that the success of the launch party I arranged for the opening of the new hotel in Zubran has resulted in such effective publicity that the place is now running at one hundred per cent occupancy, thus offering a considerable boost to your local economy both in terms of employment and increased tourism, which has additional benefits for the surrounding area.' Without looking up, she scrolled through her emails. 'But it's true that as well as the proven commercial benefits of employing my company, there are less tangible ones. I create memories for people. Memories that will last for ever. I am often privileged to be present at the happiest moments of people's lives. Anniversaries, engagements, weddings—moments that would undoubtedly always be special, but which I can make unforgettable. By recommending those doves that you consider to be of so little importance, I have probably saved his marriage. It's ironic, don't you think, that I, a self-confessed cynic about marriage, should be working to preserve one while you, a staunch supporter, mock my efforts.'

'I wasn't mocking you.'

'You mocked my business, Mal. You never took my business seriously.' There was a snap in her voice and she leaned her head back against the seat and closed her eyes. 'Sorry. This is history. I don't know why we're talking about it except that it passes the time.'

'I apologise,' he breathed. 'No one could fail to admire what you've achieved with your company.'

'Is it the "frivolous" nature of my business that disturbs you most, or the fact that I work like a man?'

'I don't know what you're talking about.' But he did know what she was talking about and his hands gripped the wheel just a little bit tighter.

'Oh come on, Mal! You like to think of yourself as progressive, but you're not comfortable with a woman who is as passionate about her work as a man would be. You don't think I should fly around the world, live out of suitcases and occasionally sleep in my office. That's what men do, isn't it? You believe that work is what a woman does until she finds a man, marries and has a family. It would be quaint if it weren't so exasperating.'

'I have no problems with your work ethic. I admire it.'

'From a distance. Even now, you can't admit the truth.'

'And what is "the truth"? Enlighten me.' They were snapping at each other, releasing the almost intolerable energy they created together in the only way open to them.

'You want a woman barefoot and pregnant in the kitchen. No opinions. No life of her own. That is why you are marrying Kalila.'

He was marrying Kalila because it was the only option left to him.

'This is a pointless conversation.'

Her glossy mouth curved into a smile. 'Men always say that when they've lost. Never "you're right" or "I screwed up", just "this is a pointless conversation". Do they give speeding tickets out here? Because if they do then you're going to get one. You seem angry. Are you angry?' She was pushing him and he realised just how easy he made that for her. It was doubly frustrating because normally the desert relaxed him.

'I'm concerned about Kalila. It's important that we make the edge of the mountains by dusk.' He slowed the speed fractionally, exasperated with himself for allowing her to wind him up. 'I know a good place to camp, but I want to set up while there is still some light.' That observation was greeted by silence.

'So no chance of reaching your bride tonight then?'

'If she is where her sister suspects she is, then no. We will have to stop for one night.' A night alone in the desert with this woman. He was greeting that prospect with almost as much enthusiasm as his impending wedding.

'So if her sister knew where she was going, why didn't she stop her?'

'She didn't know. Kalila sent her the same note she sent me. Jasmina was afraid of her father's reaction, so she contacted me instead. Which was fortunate because at least we have more to go on than we did before. She is covering for her sister. At the moment the Sheikh does not even know his daughter is not in her rooms.'

'Her father sounds like a real treasure. Better to not have one than have one who induces fear.'

It was the first time he'd ever heard her mention her father.

Mal turned his head and glanced at her, but she was looking forwards, a tiny frown between her eyes as she focused on the sand dunes that rose either side of them. 'I love how they change colour with the light. And the way the pattern changes—it's fascinating.'

'It's the combination of wind and sun.' He'd watched her fall in love with the exotic, mysterious dunes the first time round and he could still remember the delight on her face when she'd witnessed her first desert sunset. Another irony, he thought, that this woman who had been raised in a Western city should feel an affinity for the place of his birth while Kalila, with her desert heritage, found the place nothing short of repellent. 'Your father wasn't around when you were young?'

'Are we playing psychotherapy next?' She met question with question and he sighed, wondering what it took to get her to open up.

'In all the time I've known you, you've never talked about your father.'

'That's because there is nothing to say.' Her cool tone was like a wind blown straight from the Arctic, her words designed to freeze that line of questioning in mid-flow.

Mal refused to be deflected even though part of him was wondering why he was choosing to ask these questions now, when it was too late for them. 'Did he leave when you were young?' It was a personal question, and probably unadvised given his vow to avoid the personal, but nevertheless he asked it. He'd always assumed that her father was somehow responsible for her aversion to marriage but she'd never given him any detail.

'Why the sudden interest in my father? We were talking about Kalila's situation, not mine.'

'I'm just thinking it must have been hard for you growing up without a man in your life.'

'You're doing it again—assuming that a woman needs a man to survive.'

Mal breathed deeply, refusing to rise. 'That is *not* what I assume. Why are you deliberately misinterpreting my words?'

'I'm not. I just know you, Mal.'

'Maybe you don't.' He wondered how he could have been so blinkered. *She was afraid.* Why hadn't he seen that before?

'We both know you have very traditional views on the role of women.'

'Do not assume to know what I am thinking.'

'It's not hard to guess. You're marrying a woman you barely know so that you can have a traditional set-up and breed children.'

'Is it so wrong to think a child benefits from being raised in a traditional family unit?'

'I wasn't raised in a traditional family unit and I'm fine.'

No, he thought. *You're not fine.* 'I'm not saying that a child can't be fine with one parent. But family offers security.'

'You're talking rubbish. Take Kalila's father—would she be better off with a mother who teaches her to be strong and independent or a father who bullies her?' She spoke just a little too quickly. Was a little too anxious to move the conversation away from her own situation.

Mal thought of his own father. Strict, yes, and often busy, of course. But never too busy to spend time with his son. 'Your mother didn't remarry?'

'I don't know why you're going on about fathers. Kalila's has frightened her into running away and yours has pressured you to marry a woman you barely know.'

She hadn't answered his question. 'He didn't pressure me.' This was the point where he should tell her the truth about his union with Kalila but something held him back. 'We are well suited.'

'Because you give out the orders and she says yes? That's not a relationship, Mal. That's servitude. You've barely had a conversation with her. You know nothing about her likes and dislikes and you have no idea why she's run away or where she could be heading. None of that suggests an unbreakable bond.'

Their conversations had always been lively, but never before today had she been so openly antagonistic. It was as if she were trying to goad him.

'I have a great deal of respect for Kalila and I value her opinion.'

'When has she ever expressed an opinion? When has she ever actually voiced a thought that isn't yours?'

'Perhaps we think alike.'

Her beautiful mouth twisted into a wry smile. 'More likely she's afraid to tell you what she really thinks. Or perhaps she doesn't even *know* what she really thinks because she's never been allowed to find out. You need to do something about that, Your Highness. Not only is it politically incorrect to want a passive wife, it's going to bore you in five minutes.' The car bumped into a pothole and she winced. 'And while you're ruling the world, you really do need to do something about the state of your roads.'

And the state of his nerves. He was tense. On edge. *Angry.* 'This road is not my responsibility. We left Zubran half an hour ago. You are now in Arhmor and infrastructure has never been a high priority for the Sheikh.' The scenery had changed. They were approaching mountains and the road was rougher. Everything about Arhmor was rougher. 'Let's hope we don't blow a tyre. This is not somewhere to break down.'

'So instead of mending his roads, the Sheikh tries to

build his empire. I suppose that's what this marriage is about, is it? You are the wealthier state. I assume he's hoping that if you marry his daughter, you'll fix his roads for him.'

'It's true that this marriage will bring political advantages—' Mal turned the wheel to avoid another deep rut in the road '—but that is not the only reason for the marriage. Kalila is a princess with an impeccable bloodline.'

'You make her sound like breeding stock. On the other hand, I suppose that's what she is. A brood mare to produce lots of little Sultans for the future.' Her tone flippant, she turned her head and looked over her shoulder. 'Are you sure you're taking the right route? Because according to the sat nav you should have turned left back there. You should have let me drive. Everyone knows a man can't do two things at once.'

She was definitely goading him.

What he didn't understand was why. Why would she want to make this journey more difficult and unpleasant than it already was?

Mal breathed deeply, transferred his gaze to the screen and cursed softly. She was right. He'd missed an important turning. Not because he couldn't do two things at once, but because he'd been so distracted by Avery and by his impending marriage that he hadn't been concentrating. Slamming the vehicle into reverse, he took the correct route. Around them, the landscape grew steadily more bleak and barren. 'Say one word and I'll dump you by the side of the road.'

'I wouldn't dream of making a sound.' It was clear from her voice that she was enjoying his mistake and he tightened his grip on the wheel.

'You're infuriating, you know that, don't you?'

'Because I pointed out you were going the wrong way?'

'I'm perfectly capable of driving. If you want to pick a fight, you're going to have to choose a different battleground.'

'This is why our relationship ended. Because we can't be civil to each other for five minutes. The only thing we were ever really good at as a couple was fighting.'

So that was it. That was the game she was playing.

She was snapping because she was terrified of what they'd once shared. She was terrified that if she stopped snapping, something else would happen. Something far, far more dangerous.

Wondering how he could have been so dense, Mal slammed his foot on the brake and the car stopped suddenly.

Anger throbbing inside him, he turned to look at her. 'That is *not* why our relationship ended.' His voice thickened with emotion and he wondered what it was about this woman that triggered such extreme feelings. 'And we were good at a great deal more than fighting.' He saw the change in her. Saw her spine grow rigid and her breathing grow shallow.

'No, we weren't.'

'We both know *exactly* why our relationship ended, Avery, and it had nothing to do with the arguments.'

Her skin was flawless, smooth and very, very pale. Her mouth was a tight line in her beautiful face. 'There is nothing to be gained by talking about this.'

'Maybe not, but we're talking about it anyway.'

'Mal—'

'Our relationship ended because I asked you to marry me,' he said harshly. 'And you said no. *That's* why it ended.'

CHAPTER FOUR

'Stop the car!' For a fleeting second she'd tried telling her-self that it wasn't worth going over this, but her emotions were too raw for that. She was so angry that all of her was shaking. Her knees. Her hands… 'Stop the damn car, *right now.*' She was out of the door before the vehicle came to a standstill and Mal was right behind her, the slam of the door breaking the stillness of the burning air.

Theirs was the only vehicle in sight. They were alone in the spectacular open space of the desert, surrounded by shimmering dunes and the soaring mountains.

'You intend to walk from here?'

'Is that really your recollection of events? You truly be-lieve that you "asked" me to marry you?' Her hair swung across her back as she turned to confront him. Her heart was racing and she felt the heat of the sun beating down on her head. She realised that she'd left her hat in the car, but it was too late to care about that now. 'We must be existing in a parallel universe or something because I remember it *very* differently.' Right now her anger was hotter than any-thing produced by nature but underneath that pulsing anger were layers of different emotions. Pain. Desire. Sexual awareness. Feelings. *Feelings she didn't want to feel.* And he clearly didn't either if his expression was anything to go by. He was watching her with the same cautiousness he would give an enraged scorpion.

'Avery—'

'And when you think about it, that's not surprising because you never *ask* anyone anything, do you? You command. You order. You instruct.' She ticked them off on her fingers while he watched with a dangerous glint in those dark eyes.

'Are you finished?'

'I've barely started. You're so arrogant you never involve anyone else in your decisions. No wonder your virgin bride has run into the desert.'

His eyes flared dark. '*Stop* calling her that.'

'Tell me something.' Still shaking, Avery put her hands on her hips. 'Did you actually *ask* her to marry you, Mal? Or did you just book the wedding and then mention it to her in passing? Perhaps that's what's wrong here. Perhaps no one remembered to tell her she was supposed to be getting married. Did you miss her off the invitation list?'

A muscle flickered in his bronzed cheek. 'I'm the first to admit that my proposal to you went awry, but there were circumstances—'

'*Awry?* It didn't go "awry", Mal. It didn't happen. There was no proposal. There was just assumption. Lots of arrogant assumption.' All the anger and humiliation came piling back on top of her. And the terror. She'd almost lost everything. All of it. Everything she'd worked for. 'You assumed I was a sure thing. That of course I'd say yes to you because who wouldn't? You were so sure of yourself you didn't even pause to think about *my* needs, and you were so sure of me you didn't even bother to ask my opinion on the topic. And there are no circumstances that can explain or excuse your arrogance!'

'And if there were, you wouldn't listen to them.'

'The first I knew of your "proposal" was *not* when you and I had a private moment during which you asked me if I'd consider marrying you, but when one of my biggest clients rang to cancel his contract with me because he'd heard that I was no longer going to be running my company. When I asked him where that rumour had originated, he told me that he'd heard it from you. That you'd told him that once you married me I would no longer be taking on more business. Because of you, I lost clients. I could have lost the whole business. *My* business. The business I built from nothing.' The thought of how close she'd come to losing everything that mattered to her sent her spiralling into panic. 'That is what our "romance" did for me. And you wonder why I'm not romantic?'

There were lines of strain visible around his sensual mouth. 'That is not what I said to him.'

'Then what *did* you say to him because he was pretty sure of his facts when he took his business elsewhere. Important business, I might add. Business that would have led to more business. Instead I found myself explaining to some very confused people why I wasn't getting married.'

His eyes were a dark, dangerous black. 'And in doing so you humiliated me.'

'No, *you* humiliated *me*, Mal! You made me look like some brainless, witless woman who was just waiting for a rich, handsome Prince to come along and rescue her from her sad life. All those times you said you loved me for who I was. You said you loved my independence and my strength. And then you cut me off at the knees. Did you really think I'd just give up my business and marry you?'

'I thought you'd trust me. We'd been together for a year,' he said in a thickened tone. 'We were happy together.'

'We were happy until you tried to take over my life.

"Once we're married she won't have time to run your parties." Wasn't that what you said to him?'

There was a tense silence. 'Yes. But there were reasons—'

'Yes, and we both know what those reasons were. You have to be in control. You've been giving orders since you were old enough to put two words together and you don't know any different. The problem is, I'm not great at taking orders, Mal. I like to run my own life. In fact, I insist on it. Damn it, why are we even having this conversation?' Furious to feel her eyes stinging, she stomped back to the car but as she touched the door handle his hand covered hers. 'Get away from me. It's my turn to drive.'

'This conversation isn't finished.'

'It is as far as I'm concerned.'

'What happened with Richard Kingston was a misjudgement on my part, I admit it. But there were circumstances—'

'There isn't a single circumstance that would successfully excuse a man discussing his marital intentions with everyone before the woman he intended to marry.' She felt the warmth of his hand, the strength of those fingers as they stayed in contact with hers and forced herself to pull away.

'Are you crying?'

'Don't be ridiculous. I've got sand in my eyes. This is a very sandy place.'

'You're wearing sunglasses.'

'Well, clearly they're not very efficient.' Furious and miserable, Avery pulled open the door and slid inside. Her heart was pounding, her control shredded and her emotions raw. Why on earth had she decided to put herself through this? And in the desert. A place so closely entwined with

her relationship with Mal that she wasn't even able to look
at a picture of it without feeling sad.

On her first visit to Zubran she'd fallen in love. Twice.
First with the country; with the contrast between stunning beaches and the wild beauty of the ever-changing
dunes. Second, with the man. And somehow the two had
become inextricably linked so that she couldn't imagine
one without the other. He was part of this wild place and
part of the place existed within him, had bred the strength
and resilience that formed that steel core of his personality.

Her feelings for him had terrified her and they terrified
her still. And yes, that was why she'd done nothing but
snap at him from the moment she'd got into the vehicle.
The alternative was allowing that dangerous chemistry to
take hold and she couldn't do that. She *wouldn't* do that.

Avery tightened her fingers on the wheel as she drove,
every tiny part of her alive with awareness despite all her
efforts.

Next to her in the passenger seat, Mal sat sprawled,
beautiful eyes narrowed behind sunglasses as he stared
ahead.

She was silent and so was he, but that silence did nothing to defuse the tension.

An hour passed.

And another hour.

Neither of them spoke a word. And she was relieved to
be driving. Relieved to have something to focus on other
than him. Except that it didn't work like that, of course,
because no matter how much she focused on the road, she
was still aware of him, right there beside her. Within touching distance, except that she wasn't allowed to touch. And
awareness grew and grew until the air was almost too thick
to breathe. Until the desire to touch him was almost over-

whelming and she had to grip the wheel until her knuckles were white with the pressure.

This was why she wanted his marriage to go ahead, she thought savagely. Because only then would he be out of her head and out of her heart. She wasn't the sort of woman who could hold onto feelings for a married man. That would be it. She could get back to a normal life.

After what felt like hours of silence, he finally spoke. 'We'll camp by those rocks up ahead.' His tone was neutral. Devoid of emotion. 'They should offer some protection from the elements.'

She didn't need protecting from the elements. She needed protection from *him*. Or was it herself? She was no longer sure.

Confused and jittery, Avery parked and sprang from the vehicle. 'You can camp by that rock and I'll camp by the other.' Distance, she thought. She needed distance. They needn't even see each other until morning. She'd zip her tent up and she'd keep it zipped.

'There is just one tent, Avery.'

'What?' His words blew out the foundations of her fledgling plan and answered any remaining questions she had about her feelings for him. 'Just one? Why?'

'Why does that matter?' He seemed unusually interested in her reaction and she pushed away disturbing images of his muscle-packed length stretched next to hers.

'Well, for a start, it isn't exactly the done thing for a man to sleep with one woman when he is engaged to marry another. And then there's always the chance that I'll kill you in my sleep.' *If* she slept. Which seemed unlikely.

'I don't intend to sleep with you.' He leaned in and pulled a bag from the vehicle. 'Just share a tent with you. It isn't as if we haven't done it before.'

But the last time they'd been lovers. Intimate in every

way. They were both hot-tempered and stubborn and those traits had simply intensified the sexual connection between them.

Avery watched as he hauled the tent and the gear from the vehicle. 'Why didn't you bring two tents?'

'I wasn't expecting company. If you recall, you were the one who insisted on coming. Having already spread the word that I wanted a couple of nights in the desert alone, I could hardly articulate the need for a second tent.' He focused his attention on creating their camp and she forced herself to help, even though doing so brought her into close proximity with him. She tried to subdue the choking, panicky feeling in her chest at the thought of sharing that confined space with him.

He'd be sleeping with his head next to hers. His body within touching distance.

She looked at his shoulders and immediately looked away again.

What if she had one of her nightmares? What if she reached for him in her sleep?

Making a mental note to lie on her hands and stay awake until he was asleep, she helped secure the tent, working without speaking. And it was exasperating to discover that he was as competent at this as he was at everything else.

Avery gritted her teeth. She wasn't looking for things to admire about him. She didn't *want* to admire him. Not when they were about to spend a night crammed into a relatively small space.

At least it wasn't cold. She'd stay outside until the last possible moment before going into the tent. With luck, he'd be asleep by the time she joined him.

'Nice to know you can function without staff.' She watched as he lit a fire and proceeded to cook their supper. He'd thrown a rug on the ground and she knelt on it, watching as the flames flickered to life. 'So we should reach the oasis tomorrow? What if she isn't there?'

'I think she will be.'

'You could have just asked your security team to check it out.'

'If I'd done that it would have been impossible to keep this situation contained. I want to keep this as quiet as possible.'

'To protect your ego.'

'To protect my bride, at least until I've decided how best to sort this out.' He cooked without fuss, lamb with spices chargrilled over the open flame and served with rice. And because she was trying hard to make the whole experience less intimate she insisted on cooking her own, even though she did nowhere near as good a job as he did.

She burned the edges but still it tasted good and Avery ate hungrily until she caught him looking at her. Immediately her appetite vanished, as if someone had flicked a switch.

'What? It's delicious.'

'It's hardly gourmet. You eat in five star restaurants all the time and fly in celebrity chefs to cater for your parties.'

'Yes, but that's my work. This is different. There's something about food eaten outdoors in the desert. I've always loved it here.' Immediately she regretted saying it out loud because everything she'd loved about the desert was entwined with everything she loved about him. *Not* love. She corrected herself quickly. Felt. Everything she loved about the desert was entwined with everything she *felt* about him.

Because she knew he was looking at her, she kept her eyes on the view and that was no hardship because she could have stared for hours at the desert landscape that altered minute by minute under the fading light. The area he'd picked for camping was rocky, but they were still on

the border with Zubran and dunes rose ahead of her, dark
gold under the setting sun, the beauty of it holding her cap-
tivated until the sun dipped behind a mound and darkness
quickly spread over the desert.

Grateful for that darkness, she lifted her eyes to the sky
and picked a neutral topic. 'Why do the stars always seem
so much brighter out here?'

'Less pollution.' His tone short, he rose to his feet,
doused the fire and gestured to the tent. 'We need to get
some rest. I'd like to leave at dawn.'

So he didn't want to linger any more than she did. Didn't
want to prolong the time they spent together. The knowledge should have brought a feeling of relief but instead she
just felt hollow and numb.

'Dawn is fine with me.' Anything that meant less time
in the tent with him had to be good.

She wiped her bowl clean, nibbled on one of the dates
he'd left out on a plate and tried not to think about their first
trip into the desert together. It had been at the beginning
of their relationship, during those heady first months when
they'd been consumed by their feelings for each other. He'd
been so frustrated by the unrelenting demands on his time
and privacy that he'd arranged a secret trip. They'd joked
that he'd kidnapped her, but really they'd stolen time away,
as normal couples did all the time. He'd dismissed his security team. She'd left her phone behind. It was the first
time they'd really been on their own, away from the craziness of his existence and the craziness of hers.

It had been the happiest week of her life.

Thinking about it now brought a lump to her throat. The
ache in her chest felt like a solid lump and she sneaked a
glance towards him, only to find him watching her, that
dark gaze fiercely intense.

'Say it.'

'Say what?'

'Say what you are thinking.'

Avery swallowed. 'What am I thinking?'

'You are thinking of that week we spent together. Just the two of us.' His voice was rough and suddenly she couldn't breathe and the panic pressed down on her because that was *exactly* what she'd been thinking.

'Actually I was thinking how bleak it is here.'

His expression told her that he didn't believe her but he didn't push her. Instead he turned away, leaving her feeling more vulnerable than she ever had before.

Now what?

Not speaking about her feelings didn't change the fact they existed. And the thought of going into that tent—of being so close to him—kept her sitting outside long after she should have gone inside. She postponed the moment as long as possible. Postponed the moment when they'd be forced together in that cramped, confined space that was designed to force intimacy even between two people who were avoiding it.

Would she have insisted on joining him if she'd known about the sleeping arrangements? No, probably not. Self-preservation would have outweighed the guilt she felt towards Kalila.

Kalila. *He was going to marry Kalila.*

She had no idea how long she sat there. Time blurred. Misery deepened. Fatigue, the mortal enemy of optimism, caught up with her.

'Avery? You need to come inside the tent now. It's dark.' His voice was deep and sexy and she squeezed her eyes closed and tried to block out the images created by that voice.

'I'm not afraid of the dark.'

'No, you are afraid of intimacy, but intimacy is not on offer so you are perfectly safe in this tent with me.'

'I'm not afraid of intimacy.'

'Good. In that case, get in this tent before you become a tasty snack for a desert creature. Unless you'd rather I pick you up and put you here myself?'

That would be the worst of all options. She didn't want him to touch her but she knew he would make good on his threat if she didn't move, so she put her hand down on the rug to lever herself up and felt a sharp pain. 'Ow.' She snatched her hand away and there was a scuttling sound. 'What—? Ugh, Mal, something just bit me. And it rattles.'

He was by her side in an instant. The torch flashed and a scorpion scuttled under the rug.

'Not a rattlesnake—a scorpion. Good.'

'*Good?* Why is it good? From where I'm sitting it's seriously creepy. If we were playing "marry, kiss or push off a cliff", the scorpion would be the one off the cliff, I can tell you that.' Her voice rose and she hugged her hand to her chest. 'Are there any more out here?'

'Hundreds, probably. They come out at night.'

'*Hundreds?*' Horrified, she sprang at him, clinging like a monkey. 'Don't put me down.'

'Avery—'

'Whatever you do, don't put me down. I'm never touching the floor again. Do you seriously mean hundreds? Please tell me you're kidding.'

She'd forgotten how strong he was. His arms closed around her, strong, protective. She thought he might have been laughing but told herself he wouldn't dare laugh at her.

'I thought you were fine with desert wildlife.'

'I'm fine with the theory. Not so good with the reality

when it closes its jaws on me. And if you dare laugh I will kill you, Your Highness. Just a warning.'

'I'm not laughing. But I'm not going to let you forget this in a hurry.'

'I just bet you're not.' She buried her face in his neck, wondering why he had to smell so good.

'It's worth savouring. The moment Avery Scott became a damsel in distress.'

'No one will ever believe you and I will deny it until my dying breath, which may be soon if there are truly hundreds of those things out there. I'm not distressed. More freaked out. I can tell you this is the first time in my life I've jumped on a man.'

'I'm flattered you chose me,' he drawled. 'As a matter of interest, are you going to let go?'

'Are they still out there?'

'Yes.'

'Then I'm not letting go. You threatened to carry me to the tent. Go ahead.' She tightened her grip and he gave a soft curse.

'You're choking me.'

'I don't care.'

'If I die, you fall to the ground and they'll swarm all over you.'

'You have a sick sense of humour.' But she loosened her grip. 'Move, Mal! I want to be in the tent.'

'Damsels in distress don't usually give the orders. And I *was* in the tent. You were the one who chose scorpions over my company. Are you telling me that you're rethinking that choice?'

'Don't be flattered. All it means is that you're better than a scorpion. Don't make me beg.' She clung, her hands pressed to those solid shoulders. '*Are* you laughing?'

'No.'

'Good, because if you were laughing, I'd have to punch you with my good hand. My other hand hurts. Am I going to die?'

'It is rare for scorpion bites to cause fatalities.'

'Rare? So that means that sometimes people die, right?'

His hesitation was brief. 'Yes, but it's usually only in the very young or in people with health issues and you don't fall into either category.'

'That's not very reassuring. You're supposed to say, *"No, Avery, of course you're not going to die."* Why don't men ever know the right thing to say at the right moment?'

'If men said the right thing at the right moment, we'd be women.' He ducked inside the tent, lowered her onto a sleeping roll he'd laid out for himself and gently detached himself from her grip. The movement brought their faces very close together. She could feel his breath on her cheek. All she had to do was turn her head and their mouths would meet. And she didn't have to wonder how that would feel because she *knew*. And he knew, too.

Their eyes met and she saw the heat in his and knew he would see the same in hers because the chemistry was there, as powerful as ever. It sucked at her stomach and brushed over her skin, making her crave the impossible. She hadn't kissed a man since him and she missed him terribly.

It was a dangerous moment and it felt as if it lasted for ever. In reality it was less than a couple of seconds and she was about to push him away when he turned away from her, suddenly brisk and efficient.

'Do you normally react to bee stings or wasp stings?'

The only thing she reacted to was him.

Her mouth was so dry it felt as if she'd fallen face down in the desert. 'I have no idea. I've never been stung by either before.' The chemistry between them had shaken her almost as much as the scorpion bite. She felt vulnerable, and she hated feeling vulnerable. The last time she'd felt like this was when they'd split up.

'How are you feeling?'

'My hand throbs.' She squinted down at it and he hesitated for a moment and then slid back the sleeve of her shirt and studied it under the light. His fingers were strong and firm and she had to concentrate on keeping still. On not responding.

He wasn't hers any more. And she wasn't his.

Avery stared at his bent head; at the glossy dark hair that flopped over his forehead. She knew exactly how it would feel if she sank her hands into it because she'd done that. She'd trailed her mouth over his skin and tasted him. Everywhere.

As if feeling her thoughts, he lifted his head and she jerked back slightly, feeling guilty even though all she'd done was look.

The man was marrying Kalila. The fact that they seemed to barely know each other wasn't her business. The fact that Kalila had run away wasn't her business.

Studying her hand, he muttered something under his breath. 'I should have used the ultraviolet torch out there.'

'And how would that have helped?'

'There is a compound in the exoskeleton of the scorpion that causes it to glow in UV light.' He adjusted the light to get a better look. 'It means that we can see where they are. They show up as a ghostly green colour.'

Avery looked away so that she couldn't see his hand touching hers. Bronze against creamy white. Male against female. 'That is *disgusting*. How do you even know these things?'

'This is my country. It is my business to know.'

'Ghostly green scorpions.' She shuddered. 'I'm almost glad I couldn't see them. Remind me why I came?'

'Because you wanted to help Kalila. Tell me how badly it hurts.'

'I don't know—worse than a headache, better than the time I bounced off the trampoline and smashed my head on the floor of the school gym. Do you mind not frowning? Frowning means you're worried or that there is something seriously wrong. By the way, my hand feels as if it's on fire. Is that OK?'

Mal's mouth tightened. 'I should have made you come into the tent sooner.'

'I didn't want to do that.'

'And we both know why.'

There it was again. The chemistry that neither of them wanted.

'Let's not go there.'

'No.' There was a ripple of exasperation in his voice. 'But from now on you are by my side the whole time, no matter how uncomfortable that makes you feel. Stay there a moment and don't move. I'll be back soon.'

'You're leaving?' Without thinking, she reached out and grabbed his arm. 'Where are you going?' Realising what she'd just done, she let her hand drop. God, what was the matter with her? She was having a complete character transformation.

'To the car to get some ice.' He watched her, his expression revealing that he was every bit as surprised as she was. Reaching down, he closed his hand over her shoulder. 'You will be fine, *habibti*.'

Habibti.

Shock held her still because the last time he'd called her that, they'd been in bed together. Naked. Her legs tangled with his. His mouth hard on hers.

And he must have been experiencing the same memory because his eyes darkened and his gaze slid slowly to her mouth and then back to her eyes. Their whole past was in that one look.

This time she was the one to look away first.

'You're right. Of course I'll be fine,' she said quickly. 'I was just—' Clinging. Like a desperate female. She, who had never clung to anyone or anything before in her life, had clung. She didn't even want to think about what that would do to his macho ego. And she certainly didn't want to think about what it did for her reputation.

Horribly embarrassed, Avery shifted back as far as she could. 'Go and get the ice. Make sure you bring a bottle of Bollinger with it. And tell the scorpions to dine elsewhere. I'm no longer on the menu.'

'Are you sure you'll be all right? Only a moment ago you were clinging to me.'

'Clinging?' Her attempt at light-hearted laughter was relatively convincing. 'I was just trying to avoid being bitten by another scorpion. I'd rather they bit you than me.'

'Thanks.'

'If there had been a boulder handy, I would have stood on that. Anything to get above ground level. Don't take it personally. Now go. I'm thirsty.'

It was the first time he'd seen her lower her guard, even briefly.

And he'd lowered his guard too and called her *habibti* and that single word had shifted the atmosphere. He didn't know whether to be amused or offended that she considered him a bigger threat to her well-being than the scorpion.

Relieved, he thought grimly as he remembered the way he'd felt when she'd wrapped her arms around his neck. Unlocking the door, he removed ice and the first aid kit he carried everywhere, trying to block out the way it had felt to hold her. She was slender, leggy...*and she'd lost weight*.

Was that because of him?

No. That would mean she cared and he knew she didn't care.

He stood for a moment, listening to the sounds of the desert and the disturbing notes of his own thoughts. Then he cursed softly and slammed the door.

Inside the tent, she was sitting quietly. She looked shaken and a little pale but he had no way of knowing whether her reaction was a result of the scorpion bite or the pressure of being in such close contact with him.

Trying to concentrate on the scorpion bite and nothing else, Mal pressed ice to her burning hand and she flinched.

'Only you can produce ice in a desert.'

'I have a freezer unit in the vehicle.' And right at that moment he was working out ways to sit in it. Anything to cool himself down.

'Of course you do,' she murmured, 'because a Prince cannot be without life's little luxuries, even in this inhospitable terrain.'

'I suppose I should be relieved that you're feeling well enough to aggravate me.'

'I really don't need ice. You're hot, Your Highness, but not *that* hot.' But despite her flippant tone her cheeks were flushed. Was it the effects of the bite?

'Tell me how you are feeling.' And suddenly he realised just how bad this could be. They were miles from civilization. Even if he called a helicopter, it wouldn't arrive within an hour. He told himself that she was fit and healthy and not in any of the high-risk groups, but still anxiety gnawed at him because he knew that for some people the bite of the scorpion could be deadly. 'I don't carry anti-venom.'

'Well, thank goodness for small mercies because there

is no *way* I'd let you jab me with a needle and inject me with more poison.' She flinched as he moved the ice. 'That is freezing. Are you trying to give me frostbite?'

'I'm trying to stop the venom spreading. Does it hurt?'

'Not at all. I can't even feel it.' It was obvious that she was lying and he threw her a look.

'You are the most exasperating, infuriating woman I've ever met.'

'Thank you.' She smiled and that smile snagged his attention.

'What makes you think it was a compliment?'

'I take everything as a compliment unless I'm told otherwise. Am I going to die?'

'No.' Hiding his concern, he put his hand on her forehead. 'We need to get your clothes off.'

Her eyes flew open. 'You're warped, do you know that?'

'This isn't seduction. This is first aid.' And he didn't want to think about seduction. He didn't dare. His hands were firm as they stripped off her clothes and she made a feeble attempt to stop him.

'I can't let you see me naked.'

'I've already seen you naked on many occasions.' Too many occasions. She was the hottest, most beautiful woman he'd ever met and he didn't need to be in this position to be reminded of that fact.

'That was different. You weren't about to marry another woman. I don't get naked with almost married men.' She snatched at the sleeping bag and he let her cover herself but not before he'd caught a tantalizing glimpse of creamy skin. A glimpse that tested his self-control more than it had ever been tested before.

It was a struggle to focus on what he was doing. 'I have to cool you down and you need to stop snuggling inside that sleeping bag because you're overheating.' He poured cool water on a cloth and held it against her head. 'Females tend to have a more severe reaction because of their body mass.'

There was a dangerous gleam in her eyes. 'Are you calling me fat?'

'Did I mention the word fat?'

'You said "mass". Don't use the word "mass" in relation to my body.'

'Even if I tell you it's because you have a smaller body mass?' He didn't want to be amused. He didn't want to feel anything for this woman. 'Be silent. You need to rest.'

'I can't rest with you this close.'

He rubbed his fingers over his forehead, exhausted by the drain on his self control. It was fortunate that both of them were too principled to give in to it.

'I'm watching you for any adverse reaction.'

'Well, stop watching me. It feels creepy.' She rolled onto her side, but a moan escaped her. 'How long am I going to feel like this, Mal?' The tremor in her voice concerned him more than anything because he knew how tough she was.

'You feel bad?'

'No, I feel great.' Her words were muffled by the pillow. 'I just want to know how long this great feeling is going to last so that I can make the most of it. How long?'

'Hours, *habibti*.' He hesitated for a moment and then allowed himself to stroke her hair away from her face, telling himself that touching her was all about comfort and nothing else. 'Possibly a bit longer.'

'I was stupid. You must be furious with me.'

If only. 'I'm not furious.'

'Then try harder. It would make it easier if you were furious.'

Mal gave a cynical smile because right at that moment he doubted anything would make it easier. He placed his fingers on her wrist. 'Your pulse is very fast.'

'Well, that's nothing to do with you, so don't go flattering yourself. Scorpions always get me going.'

'It's the venom. You need to tell me how you're feeling. If necessary I'll call the helicopter and have us airlifted out of here.'

'No way. We need to find your virgin bride.'

Mal cursed under his breath and reached into his first aid kit for a bandage. '*Stop* calling her that.'

'Sorry.' She turned slightly, opened one eye and peeped at him. 'Are you angry yet?'

'No, but I'm getting there. Keep it up.'

She grinned weakly. 'I bet the scorpion is angry, too. I flung him across the ground. Horrible creature.'

'Actually they play a critical role in the ecosystem, consuming other arthropods and even mice and snakes.'

'Too much information.'

'They can control how much poison they inject into you. I think you got away lightly.'

'So does that mean he liked me or he didn't like me? Ow—*now* what are you doing?'

'I'm bandaging the bite and lifting your arm. I want to slow the spread of the venom. If this doesn't work, I'll have to call the helicopter.'

'Could we stop calling it venom? And honestly, Mal, it's fine. Stop fussing. Can we take the ice off now? It's cold.'

'That's the idea.'

'Scorpions don't like their food chilled?'

But she didn't feel cold to touch. She was boiling-hot and her arm was burning. 'Have you ever suffered an allergic reaction to anything in the past?'

'No, nothing. I'm as healthy as a horse.'

Mal felt a rush of exasperation that they hadn't avoided this situation. 'Why didn't you come into the tent sooner?'

'Because then we would have killed each other.' Her

response was glib, but her smile faltered. 'Sorry. And this time I really am apologising.'

'Apologising for what? For being aggravating? That is nothing new and you've never felt the need to apologise before.'

'For messing everything up,' she muttered. 'For making things harder for you. I shouldn't have come on this trip. I was worried about Kalila and I thought I could help but I haven't helped and it was all my fault anyway.' Her apology was as sweet as it was unexpected and he felt something squeeze inside his chest.

'I am touched that you cared enough to come,' he breathed. 'And you will be able to talk to Kalila and persuade her to confide in you, which is important given that I have failed so miserably to deliver in that area.' And he blamed himself for that. For being unapproachable, for assuming that just because his bride to be hadn't said anything, it meant that everything was fine.

They had no relationship, he thought bleakly, and it was impossible not to compare that with the feelings he and Avery shared.

'You'll make a perfect couple. I'm sure you'll be very happy. And I mean that. I'm not being sarcastic. She's very sweet and she won't drive you crazy. That's always good in a marriage.' Her voice was barely audible and she turned her head, the movement dislodging her hair from the plait. It poured over her shoulders like honey and he stared down at the silken mass, fighting the urge to sink his hands into it. Once, he'd had the right to do that. And he'd done it. All the time. It had been the most physical relationship of his life.

'Right now I am not thinking of Kalila.'

'Don't, Mal.' Her voice was muffled. 'Don't do this.'

Was this the moment to be honest? He hesitated,

wrenched apart by the conflict between duty and his own needs. And honesty would just worsen the situation, wouldn't it? 'This marriage with Kalila—'

'Will be good. If she's having second thoughts then it's because you haven't tried hard enough. You can be charming when you want to be. Of course the rest of the time you're aggravating and arrogant, but don't show her that side of you for a while and it will be fine.' Her eyes were closed, her eyelashes long and thick against her pale cheeks.

Mal stared down at her, unable to think of a single time when he'd seen Avery vulnerable. It just wasn't a word he associated with her. But tonight—yes, tonight she was vulnerable. He wanted to hold her but he didn't dare take the risk. He wasn't convinced he'd let her go.

Instead he settled for sitting close to her. 'Tell me why you avoided my calls.' Still worried about the bite, he tightened the bandage as much as he dared.

'I was super-busy.'

'You are the most efficient woman I know. If you'd wanted to answer my calls, you could have done. When we parted company I thought we would remain friends.' He should have been thinking about his bride-to-be, but all he could think about was the relationship he'd lost.

'I'm too busy for friends. About this scorpion—' as always when a subject became uncomfortable, she shifted direction '—he only bit me once. Should I be offended? Does that mean he didn't like the way I tasted? Or am I like expensive caviar—better consumed in small amounts?'

He didn't want to think about the way she tasted. Couldn't allow himself to. Frustration made his voice rougher than he intended. 'I am going to give you a couple of tablets and then you're going to rest.' *And stop talking.*

'I don't take tablets. I'm a drug-free zone.'

'You'll take these. And if the rash on your arm hasn't calmed down in an hour or so, I'm going to fly you out of here.' And maybe that would be the best thing for both of them. Reaching into his bag, he found the tablets in the supplies he carried and handed them to her with a drink of water, relieved when she swallowed the pills without question or argument but at the same time concerned because it was so unlike her not to question and argue. 'If you feel bad, I can call the helicopter now.'

'No.' Her eyes drifted shut again. 'I want to stay. I need to be with you.'

The atmosphere snapped tight. Mal felt a weight on his chest. How many times had he waited for her to say those words? And she said them now, when his life was already set on a different course. Was that why she'd picked this moment? Because she knew he couldn't act on the emotion that simmered between them? *I need to be with you.* From any other woman those words would have felt oppressive. From Avery they felt like victory. A victory that was too little, too late. 'You need to be with me? You are telling me this now?'

'Yes.' Her voice was barely audible. 'I need to be there when you find her. I need to talk Kalila into marrying you. It's the best thing for all of us.'

CHAPTER FIVE

SHE dreamed of the desert. Only this time when she dreamed of the Prince he was holding her and she couldn't walk away because he held her close, refusing to let her go.

Trapped.

She struggled slightly but she was held in a strong grip.

'Shh. It's just a dream. Go back to sleep.'

The deep male voice lifted her from sleep to semi-wakefulness and she realised that Mal was holding her. It was still dark and she didn't know which frightened her more—the realisation that she felt truly terrible, or the feeling that came from being held by him. Her head was on his chest and she could feel the slow, steady thud of his heart. She knew she should pull away, but she didn't.

She'd planned to sleep in the furthest corner of the tent but here he was, lying next to her, holding her. And it felt good.

Too good.

She could feel the brush of his leg against hers and the warmth of his body as he held her in the curve of his arm. The faint glow of light from the torch simply increased the feeling of intimacy.

'For God's sake Mal, move over,' she muttered, 'you're in my personal space.'

'I'm worried about you.'

Her stomach flipped because no one had ever worried about her in her life before. 'Don't be. I don't like the idea you're waiting for me to drop dead. And you certainly don't need to hold me.'

'You're the one holding me.' He kept his eyes closed, those dark lashes inky black against his cheek. 'You did it in your sleep, because you just can't accept help when you're awake.'

'That's because I don't need help when I'm awake.'

'Right. And I suppose you didn't "need help" last night when you used me as a climbing frame?'

'That was different. We were invaded by scorpions and if it's all right with you I'd like to forget about last night.' She wanted to forget all of it, especially this. She wondered why he was still holding her when the safe and sensible thing to do would have been to let her go.

'How long have you been having bad dreams?'

'I don't have bad dreams.'

'You had a bad dream. That's how you ended up clinging to me.'

Embarrassment washed over her like burning liquid. 'If I had a bad dream last night then it must have been a scorpion-venom-induced nightmare.' She tried to pull away but he was stronger than she was and he held her tightly.

'It wasn't scorpions you were talking about in your sleep.'

She'd been talking in her sleep? Could this get any worse? She wanted to ask if she'd spoken his name, but didn't want to hear the answer and anyway it was impossible to concentrate with him holding her. It felt dangerously familiar.

'That's another scorpion venom thing—' Her cheek was still against his chest and she could feel hard muscle through the softness of his T-shirt. 'Check out Wikipedia.

I bet it will say something about nightmares. And I'm well and truly awake now, so you can let me go.'

He didn't. 'Go back to sleep.'

He expected her to sleep while he was holding her? She could have pulled away, of course, but she didn't. *Couldn't*. This was the way she wanted to sleep. Holding each other. Not wanting to be parted even in sleep. And she'd longed for it so much over the long, barren months they'd been apart. This was the last time they'd ever hold each other and she didn't want it to end. Without warning, her eyes started to sting. 'I don't need you to fuss over me.'

'You never need anything, do you, Avery Scott?' His voice was soft in the darkness and she squeezed her eyes tightly so that the tears didn't fall. She couldn't believe she was actually crying. She could just imagine what her mother would say to that.

'Sometimes I pretend to need someone, just to stroke a masculine ego.'

'I doubt you have ever stroked a man's ego in your life. Knifed it, possibly.'

She smiled against his chest, safe in the knowledge that he couldn't see her. 'Good job yours is robust.'

'Are you smiling?'

'No. What is there to smile about? I'm scorpion chow.' And she was a mess. The pain in her hand was nothing compared to the pain in her heart and he must have sensed her feelings because she felt his hand stroke her hair. Just the slight brush of his fingers, but it was enough to make her tense and he must have felt that too because he stilled, as if aware he'd crossed a line.

'Go back to sleep, Avery. And, just this once, don't fight me. A woman doesn't have to be in charge one hundred per cent of the time.' His soft voice melted everything hard inside her.

When they'd parted it had almost broken her. Being with him had threatened everything she'd built. She should be pulling away from him, but what she wanted to do was bury her face in his neck, touch her mouth to his skin and use her tongue and her lips to drive him wild.

Picturing Kalila in her head, she eased away from him and this time he let her go.

'I'm still in charge,' she whispered back. 'I just let you hold me because it feeds your manly ego.'

'You're all heart.'

Well, that was true, she thought bleakly as she turned on her side with her back to him. It was a good description because, right now, it was the only part of herself of which she was aware and it was filled to the brim with her feelings for him.

Even with her back to him, she could feel him watching her and she squeezed her eyes shut and refused to let herself turn and look at him.

Gritting her teeth, she resigned herself to a night without sleep.

She was alone in the tent when she woke.

Outside she could hear noises. Mal was up and dismantling their camp.

Avery lay for a moment, staring up at the canvas, remembering the night before in excruciating detail.

Muttering a soft curse, she sat upright. The bite on her hand had calmed down overnight and was now nothing more than a red mark. If only all her other feelings had faded so easily. She didn't want to think about the way he'd held her. She definitely didn't want to think about what she might have said when she'd talked in her sleep.

Grabbing her bag, she cleansed her face with one of the wipes she always carried, applied suncream and minimal make-up and scooped her hair into a ponytail. Then she tugged a fresh shirt out of her bag and changed quickly.

That was the easy part. The hard part was leaving the tent.

Facing him, after what had happened the night before.

'Coffee—' Mal handed her a small cup of strong coffee and she took it with a murmur of thanks, avoiding eye contact as she sipped.

'So you're ready to move out?'

'Whenever you are. How are you feeling?'

'Fine! Never better.' And never more embarrassed. She couldn't decide whether to pretend it hadn't happened or talk it down.

'Let me see.' He took her hand in his and somehow she resisted the impulse to snatch it away.

'It's settled down.' Which was more than could be said for her pulse rate. Could he feel it? *Could he feel what he was doing to her?* 'How's the scorpion feeling this morning? Perky?'

His mouth flickered at the corners. 'Deprived, I should think. He only got to take a single bite. I'm sure it was nowhere near enough.'

Her eyes skidded to his and then away again. 'Well, that's all he's getting.' She tugged her hand away from his and finished her coffee. 'I'll take the tent down.'

'No. I want you to rest your hand. I'll do it.' He strode away from her and Avery breathed out slowly. She felt weird and she didn't know if it was the after-effects of the scorpion bite or the after-effects of a night spent close to Mal.

He had the tent down in record time and the site cleared while Avery stood, eyeing the ground for more scorpions and wondering whether or not to say something. 'Listen—' she watched as he threw the tent into the trunk, distracted

as the powerful muscles in his shoulders rippled and flexed
'—about last night—'

'Which part of last night?'

'The part when I—' She cleared her throat. 'The part when I wasn't quite myself.'

'Was that the moment when you clung to me, or the moment you begged me not to leave you?'

'I didn't beg. And I didn't cling.' She emptied the dregs of her coffee onto the ground. 'Not exactly.'

'You needed me. But I can understand that it's hard for you to admit to needing anyone.' There was an edge to his voice that she didn't understand because surely they were way past this in their relationship.

'I didn't need you, but if it suits you to believe that then fine. I wish I'd never mentioned it. How long until we find your bride?' The sooner the better as far as she was concerned. Suddenly she wished she hadn't allowed her conscience to push her into this trip. No matter what she'd said to Kalila, if the girl had chosen to leg it into the desert that was ultimately her responsibility, wasn't it? Nothing was worth this additional stress.

'It is about a two-hour drive from here.' He slung the rest of their gear into the vehicle and sprang into the driver's seat.

Two hours and that would be it, she thought numbly. He'd find his bride. They'd sort things out. Mal would marry her. And all she'd ever be to him was a past he wanted to forget.

They'd see each other at the occasional high profile party. They'd be polite and friendly and formal. And in time the pain would fade.

She rubbed her hand over her chest.

He caught the movement and frowned slightly but Avery

ignored his quizzical look and walked round to the passenger side.

This time, instead of arguing, they made the journey in silence but it didn't seem to make a difference. She was painfully conscious of him, her eyes drawn to every tiny movement. The flex of his thigh as he drove, the strength of his hands on the wheel. The atmosphere was so tense and loaded that when they finally pulled in to the camp Avery was the first out of the car. She wanted to get this done. She *had* to get this done.

'Stay there. I'll ask a few questions and try to find out where she is. You'll draw too much attention to yourself.' Without waiting for his response, she walked towards the tent that doubled as 'reception' but, before she reached it, she noticed the slim figure of a girl hurrying, head down, into a tent at the far side of the camp.

Kalila?

Sure it was her, Avery walked straight towards the tent where she'd seen the girl disappear.

'Have you seen her?' Mal was right behind her and she scowled at him.

'I don't know. I think so, but presumably she doesn't want to see you or she would have gone to you in the first place. I think you should wait in the car.'

'Am I so fearsome?' Those ebony eyes glittered down at her and just for a moment she felt the connection, powerful and unsettling. *Yes, he was fearsome*. Because of him she'd almost lost everything she'd worked to build.

'I have no idea what she thinks about you. And I'm not going to find out if you're standing there scowling. Go and take a stroll in the desert for a few minutes.' Pulling aside the flap of the tent, she stepped inside. And stared in dismay because there, in the centre of the tent was Kalila.

And wrapped around her was a man. A man who was most certainly *not* her bridegroom to be.

Avery absorbed the undeniable evidence that yet another relationship had crashed and burned. Despite her own unshakeable cynicism, this time she was shocked. Of all the scenarios that had played around in her head, this had not been among them. Or maybe she hadn't allowed herself to think that the marriage might not go ahead. It had to go ahead. It *had* to.

Panic rippled through her and this time she didn't know if it was for herself or Kalila.

Maybe if Mal didn't see—if she could just talk to Kalila—do *something*—

She tried to back out of the tent before the couple noticed her and almost tripped over Mal, who was right behind her. Her retreat blocked by his powerful body, she tried to thrust him back. 'It's not her. My mistake.'

He stood firm, refusing to budge, his handsome face blank of expression as he contemplated the scene in front of him. There was no visible sign of emotion, but it wasn't hard to guess his feelings and her heart squeezed.

Damn. It wasn't even as if she believed in happy endings. But to have the ending before the beginning was particularly harsh. Whatever his reasons, he'd wanted this marriage to work.

She wanted to cover his eyes, to push him away, to catch his illusions in her bare hands before they hit the ground and shattered. But it was already too late for that.

In the circumstances, his control surprised her. There was no cursing or explosion of possessive temper. Instead he just stood, legs braced apart as he watched in silence. Everything about him screamed power and Avery felt her breath catch because most of the time she thought of him as a man first and Prince second but right now he was very much the Prince.

Clearly Kalila thought so too because as she caught sight of him she dragged herself out of the arms of her lover so quickly she almost fell. 'Oh no!'

Mal walked past Avery into the tent, his dark gaze fixed intently on the man who had been kissing Kalila. 'And you are—?'

'No! I won't let you touch him!' Her tone infused with drama and desperation, Kalila plastered herself in front of her lover—*was he a lover?*—and Avery braced herself. No doubt there would be a battle for masculine supremacy. Holding her breath, she waited for him to face Mal, man to man, but instead he stayed firmly behind the Princess and then prostrated himself.

'Your Highness—'

Avery's brows rose because she'd expected fists, not fawning. Astonished, her gaze flickered to Mal and their gazes briefly connected. She subdued a ridiculous urge to laugh and then realised that there was nothing funny about this situation. Mal was desperate for this marriage to go ahead. He would fight for Kalila, she was sure of it.

'Get up.' Mal issued the command through clenched teeth and the man stumbled upright, but stayed behind Kalila with his head bowed.

Avery watched in disbelief. What woman in her right mind would choose that cowering wimp over Mal? Not that she wanted to see them fight, but surely he should at least look his adversary in the eye and take control. Where was the strength? Where was courage?

Nowhere, apparently, because the man, scarlet-faced, continued to stare at the floor while Kalila sent him an adoring glance. In the end it was Kalila who braced her

YOUR PARTICIPATION IS REQUESTED!

Dear Reader,

Since you are a lover of romance fiction – we would like to get to know you!

Inside you will find a short Reader's Survey. Sharing your answers with us will help our editorial staff understand who you are and what activities you enjoy.

To thank you for your participation, we would like to send you 2 books and 2 gifts – **ABSOLUTELY FREE!**

Enjoy your gifts with our appreciation,

Pam Powers

SEE INSIDE FOR READER'S SURVEY

For Your Romance Reading Pleasure...

We'll send you 2 books and 2 gifts
ABSOLUTELY FREE
just for completing our Reader's Survey!

YOUR READER'S
"THANK YOU" FREE G̲[...]̲LUDE:
▶ 2 Harlequin Pre[...]ks
▶ 2 lovely surprise g[...]

▶ **PLEASE FILL IN THE CIRCLES COMPLETELY TO RESPOND**

1) What type of fiction books do you enjoy reading? (Check all that apply)
- ○ Suspense/Thrillers
- ○ Action/Adventure
- ○ Modern-day Romances
- ○ Historical Romance
- ○ Humour
- ○ Paranormal Romance

2) What attracted you most to the last fiction book you purchased on impulse?
- ○ The Title
- ○ The Cover
- ○ The Author
- ○ The Story

3) What is usually the greatest influencer when you <u>plan</u> to buy a book?
- ○ Advertising
- ○ Referral
- ○ Book Review

4) How often do you access the internet?
- ○ Daily ○ Weekly ○ Monthly ○ Rarely or never.

5) How many NEW paperback fiction novels have you purchased in the past 3 months?
- ○ 0 - 2
- ○ 3 - 6
- ○ 7 or more

YES! I have completed the Reader's Survey. Please send me the 2 FREE books and 2 FREE gifts (gifts are worth about $10) for which I qualify. I understand that I am under no obligation to purchase any books, as explained on the back of this card.

❏ I prefer the regular-print edition
106/306 HDL FNP6

❏ I prefer the larger-print edition
176/376 HDL FNP6

FIRST NAME   LAST NAME

ADDRESS

APT.#   CITY

STATE/PROV.   ZIP/POSTAL CODE

▶ DETACH AND MAIL CARD TODAY!

HP-SUR-12/12
© 2012 HARLEQUIN ENTERPRISES LIMITED
® and ™ are trademarks owned and used by the trademark owner and/or its licensee. Printed in the U.S.A.

The Reader S   How It Works:

Accepting your 2 free b[...]valued at approximately $10.00) places you under no obligation to buy anything. You may keep the books and gift[...]ement marked "cancel." If you do not cancel, about a month later we'll send you 6 additional books and bill you just $[...]edition or $4.80 each for the larger-print edition in the U.S. or $4.99 each for the regular-print edition or $5.49 each fo[...]da. That is a savings of at least 13% off the cover price. It's quite a bargain! Shipping and handling is just 50¢ per b[...]k in Canada.* You may cancel at any time, but if you choose to continue, every month we'll send you 6 more books, wi[...]the discount price or return to us and cancel your subscription.

BUSINESS REPLY MAIL
FIRST-CLASS MAIL   PERMIT NO. 717   BUFFALO, NY

POSTAGE WILL BE PAID BY ADDRESSEE

THE READER SERVICE
PO BOX 1341
BUFFALO NY 14240-8571

NO POSTAGE
NECESSARY
IF MAILED
IN THE
UNITED STATES

If offer card is missing write to: The Reader Service, P.O. Box 1867, Buffalo, NY 14240-1867 or visit: www.ReaderService.com

shoulders and faced the man she was supposed to be marrying.

'I won't let you lay a finger on him.'

'I have no intention of touching him,' Mal drawled, 'but an introduction would be appropriate at this point, don't you think?'

'This is Karim.' Kalila's voice was a terrified squeak. 'He's my bodyguard.'

'You *have* to be kidding.' Avery stared at the cowering man. 'Your *bodyguard*? But—' She caught Mal's single warning glance and broke off in mid sentence. 'Sorry. I'm not saying anything. Nothing at all. I'm totally silent on the subject. Mute. Lips are sealed.'

'If only,' Mal breathed, returning his attention to the couple in front of him. 'So your "bodyguard" appears to be taking his responsibilities extremely seriously. Presumably he was wrapped that closely around you to protect you from flying bullets?' His biting sarcasm drew an uncomfortable glance from the other man but he didn't speak.

The talking was left to Kalila, who was every bit as red faced as the man next to her. 'Wh-what are you doing here, Your Highness?'

'I was searching for my bride-to-be,' Mal said softly, 'to find out why she'd run away. But apparently I have my answer.'

What?

Braced to defuse serious tension, Avery stared at him. Was that it? *Was that all he was going to say?*

Kalila seemed equally taken aback. 'Your Highness, I can explain—'

'You can call me Mal. I believe I've told you that on more than one occasion. And the situation doesn't merit any further explanation.'

Why wasn't he fighting?

Avery wondered if he had heatstroke. *Something* had affected his brain, that was for sure.

Kalila was still clasping the bodyguard's hand tightly. Probably to stop him running away, Avery thought. 'I can't believe you came looking for me. Why would you do that?'

'Because he's a decent person and he was worried about you,' Avery snapped and then caught Mal's eye again. 'All *right*. It's just that you're not saying anything and it's really hard to stay silent—'

'Try,' Mal advised silkily and Avery clamped her jaws shut. Without even realising it, she'd moved closer to him so that now all she had to do was reach out her hand and she'd be touching him. And she wanted to touch him. *She wanted to touch him so badly.*

'We came looking for you because naturally we were concerned that you might be in danger. But I can see that you're fine.' Mal was calm and composed and Avery resisted the temptation to poke him to check he was actually still alive. Surely he should be seething with anger? Burning up with raw jealousy?

Or perhaps he was just in shock. Yes, that had to be it. Shock.

But if he wasn't careful the moment to act would have passed. And if he wasn't capable of taking action, then she'd do it for him. 'What Mal is trying to say is that—'

'I can't marry you, Your Highness.' Kalila blurted the words out. 'It's too late.'

Avery closed her eyes. 'Of course it's not too late! Honestly, you shouldn't make hasty decisions, Kalila. You need some time to think about this. And when you've talked it through I'm sure you'll change your mind because Mal is a fantastic catch for any girl and you're really lucky.'

'This is nothing to do with His Royal Highness—' Kalila avoided Mal's gaze '—I don't want to be the Sultan's wife. I'd be hopeless. I'm shy and I'm not an interesting person.'

Avery gave Mal a look, expecting him to contradict her and when he didn't, she took over. 'That is not true at all. Just because you're shy doesn't mean you're not interesting.'

'You have no idea how hard I find it in crowds. And the Prince doesn't want to marry a mute. He gets really impatient when I don't speak.'

'Of course he doesn't!' Avery drove her elbow into Mal's ribs to prompt him to speak but he remained ominously silent. 'Mal loves you just the way you are.' Her less than subtle hint went unrewarded.

'He doesn't love me,' Kalila stammered, her face scarlet, 'he loves *you.*'

Silence filled the tent.

Avery felt as if someone was choking her. She lifted her hand to her throat, but there was nothing there, of course. Nothing she could loosen to help her breathing. 'That isn't true. He loves *you.* He asked you to marry him!'

'He asked you first.'

Oh, for crying out loud. 'No, he didn't, actually.' Avery spoke through her teeth. 'I don't know what you've heard, but that was all a big misunderstanding. You don't know the details.' *And why wasn't Mal telling her the truth? Putting her right?*

'I do know the details. I was there. I heard what he said. I heard him have a row with that horrible man who runs that oil production company and thinks he's irresistible—'

Avery frowned, confused. 'Richard?'

'Yes, him. He told Mal that you were planning his party and he was going to have you as a bonus. Mal was so angry he punched him. And when he dragged him out of the dirt where he'd knocked him, he told him that he was going to marry you and that you wouldn't be able to run any parties for him, now or in the future, personal or otherwise.'

Avery discovered that her mouth was open.

Slowly, she turned her head to look at Mal, waiting for him to deny it, but still he said nothing. Apart from a faint streak of colour across his cheekbones, he made no response.

Confusion washed over her. She knew he hadn't loved her. He'd proposed to Kalila within weeks of them parting. 'You misunderstood.'

'I was there,' Kalila said quietly. 'There was no misunderstanding. It's the only time anyone has seen Mal lose his cool.'

'Well, Richard can be a very annoying person. I've almost lost my cool with him a million times.' Dismissing the incident as a display of male jealousy, Avery forced herself back to the immediate situation. 'He was obviously trying to wind Mal up and he succeeded, which is why he said all that about marriage… That doesn't have any impact on what is going on here. Of course he wants to marry you. We've just spent two days chasing through the desert trying to find you.'

Kalila looked at her steadily. 'Together.'

'Not together *as such*—' Avery felt her cheeks darken as she thought about their night in the tent '—just because that's the way it worked out.'

'He went straight to you with the problem because he loves you and trusts you.'

'He came straight to me because he thought I might know where you were! That doesn't mean he loves me. He doesn't! I'd be a terrible Sultan's wife. Actually I'd be a terrible wife, full stop. I don't have any of the qualities necessary, in particular the fundamental one of actually *wanting* to get married.' She was stammering, falling over her words like a child practising public speaking for the first time, exasperated by Kalila's insistence that Mal loved her. 'We're just friends. And not even that, most of the time.'

Mal remained silent.

Why on earth didn't he *speak?* And why couldn't Kalila stop talking?

'You're the only woman he's ever loved,' she said. 'He was just marrying me for political reasons. Because it was agreed between our families.'

'Well, political reasons are as good a justification for marriage as any. I've known many fine, successful marriages that started from a lot less than that—'

'Avery—' Mal's voice was soft and he didn't turn his head in her direction '—you've said enough.'

'Enough? I've barely started. And you're not saying anything at all! Honestly, the pair of you just need to—' Her voice tailed off as he lifted his hand and she wondered how it was that he could silence her with a single subtle gesture that was barely visible to others.

Kalila bit her lip. 'You don't need to worry about it. It doesn't bother me that you don't love me, Your Highness. I don't love you either. It says something that we've known each other for years and we've barely spoken. To be honest—'

'*Don't* be honest,' Avery said quickly, interrupting before Kalila said something that couldn't be unsaid. 'Honesty is an overrated quality in certain circumstances and this is *definitely* one of them.'

'I need to say how I feel.' Kalila stuck her chin out and Avery sighed.

'Oh go on then, if you must, but you're not displaying any of the cardinal signs of shyness, I can tell you that. From where I'm standing you'd be fine at a public gathering. The challenge would be allowing someone else to get a word in edgeways.'

Kalila ignored her. 'Mal is gorgeous, of course. But he's also intimidating.'

'That's just his Prince act and he has to do that, otherwise he'd be mobbed by well-wishers, but underneath that frown he's a really gentle, cuddly guy—' Avery caught the lift of his dark eyebrows and cleared her throat 'Well, perhaps not *gentle*, exactly, but very decent. Principled. Good. And—'

'All right, that's enough. We're going to discuss this now and then the subject will never be raised again.' Finally Mal took charge and Avery relaxed slightly.

About time too.

Mal's eyes were fixed on his bride. 'You don't want to be married to a man who will become the Sultan?'

Avery gave a growl of exasperation. What was he *doing*? That was hardly going to persuade Kalila, was it? And, as if to prove her right, Kalila shook her head vigorously.

'No. I'll be hopeless, especially at all those meet and greet things you do. Parties.' She shuddered. 'The very worst of me would be on display.'

Giving up on Mal, Avery intervened again. 'Did your father tell you that? Because honestly, it's nonsense. You have a lovely personality. Stop putting yourself down! You have plenty to talk about. And anyway, all you have to do at these meet and greet gatherings is get people to talk about themselves. That's what I do all the time at my parties. I barely have to say a word. It's stopping people talking about themselves that's usually the problem, not starting them.'

'I'm nothing like you.'

'I know! And that's what makes you perfect for Mal. And you *are* perfect for him.' Avery beamed at her, hoping that her body language would reinforce the positive message. 'The moment I saw the two of you together, I knew you were a match made in heaven.'

Kalila's startled glance made her realise she might have been a bit too enthusiastic. Afraid that her response might have a counter-effect, she moderated her tone. 'There is no "right" personality for being a Sultan's bride. You'll be friendly and approachable and a real hit.'

'But I'll hate it. I will dread every moment.'

'It will get easier with time, I'm sure. I have some girls working for me who were pretty shy when they started and now I can't shut them up. Honestly, Kalila, you're going to be a huge success and very popular. I wish you'd just talked to someone about this instead of running away.'

'I did. I talked to you! You were my inspiration.'

Avery gulped. Heat rushed into her cheeks as she remembered Mal saying something similar. 'Me?'

'Yes. You told me to face my fears and that's what I did. I can't thank you enough.'

Avery made a vow never to give another person advice again as long as she lived. 'I was speaking metaphorically. I didn't actually mean for you to run off into the desert just because you're afraid of it.'

'That wasn't the fear I was facing.' Kalila lifted her chin, surprisingly stubborn. 'The fear I was facing—am still facing—is my father. All my life he's used fear to control me. I've never been allowed to do what I wanted to do. I'm not even allowed to express an opinion.'

Sympathy was eclipsed by her own feelings of panic as Avery watched the situation unravel. 'Your father doesn't even know you're gone yet. Everyone has been covering for you. You haven't actually faced him. You've avoided him.'

'I've faced the fear of him. For the first time in my life, I've done something I know will incur his disapproval. I know there will be consequences and I'm willing to take them. I knew that if I ran off he would never forgive me. He will not have me back in his house, under his roof. I will no longer be his daughter.' Kalila clasped her hands together nervously. 'And that's what I want.'

'Well then, that's perfect, because soon you can be Mal's wife. This doesn't mean you can't marry the Prince. I'm sure there's a way round this that is going to be fine for everyone—' Her voice tailed off because Kalila was staring at her in disbelief and Avery realised how crazy she must sound. Apart from admitting that the last thing in the world she wanted was to be the Sultan's wife, the woman was clearly obsessed with her bodyguard. There was no way on this planet Mal would marry her now. How could he? And truly, she wouldn't want that for him, would she? She, who knew how badly so many marriages ended, would never want one to start in such inauspicious circumstances.

Avery's shoulders slumped. She stole a glance at Mal but he seemed maddeningly calm about the whole thing.

'So this is what you want, Kalila?' His blunt question brought colour pouring into Kalila's cheeks.

'Yes. I'm in love with Karim. I just want to live with him quietly.' She gave her shrinking beau a trembling smile. 'For ever. Happily ever after. I feel so happy.'

'I feel so sick,' Avery muttered but Mal ignored her.

'Fine. If you're sure that's what you want, then I'll make that happen. If your father won't approve the match then you can live in Zubran under my protection. You can have your happy ever after, Kalila, with my compliments.'

'"*You can have your happy ever after*"'! What sort of romantic claptrap is that? Have you gone totally mad?' Exasperated and upset for him, Avery followed Mal as he strode from the tent towards the desert. Her head was in a spin. 'You didn't even bother trying to talk her out of it.

If anything you made it easy for her by offering her sanctuary. Why didn't you just offer to conduct the ceremony while you were at it?'

Not only did she not understand it, but Mal seemed in no hurry to explain himself.

'Drop it, Avery.'

'Drop it?' She virtually had to run to keep pace with him. 'Sorry, but did we or did we not just spend two days roughing it in the desert in order to find Kalila and persuade her not to run away?'

'Certainly the intention was to find her. And we did that. Thank you for your assistance.'

Avery gave a murmur of frustration. She opened her mouth to ask him if the sun had gone to his head but he was already several strides ahead of her and she could see that he was angry.

Well, of course he was angry.

He'd found Kalila with another man.

Perhaps that explained his reaction, or lack of it. He was too gutted to respond. And too hurt to discuss it with her now.

She tried to imagine how he must feel, but as someone who had never seen marriage as an attractive option she honestly didn't have a clue. In his position she would have been rejoicing at the narrow escape, but of course he wasn't going to feel that way. He'd wanted this marriage. And as for the business with Richard—

And everything Kalila had said about Mal being in love with her—

Avery stared after him, Kalila's words in her head.

He hadn't been in love with her. She'd presented him with a challenge, that was all. They'd had fun together.

How could he have been in love? The moment they'd broken up he'd become engaged to another woman. He'd started planning his wedding. Those weren't the actions of a man in love.

She glanced towards the car and then back towards his rapidly vanishing figure.

'Damn and blast.' How could she leave him on his own? When he hurt, she hurt. It was like being physically connected and it was a bond she'd been trying to break for longer than she cared to remember.

Muttering under her breath, Avery strode after him, tugging the brim of her hat down over her eyes to shield herself from the blaze of the desert sun and the scrutiny of curious tourists. *Relationships,* she thought. *Why did anyone bother?* Her mother was right. They were nothing but trouble.

As she approached him, she tried to work out what to say.

Better now than in ten years' time...

Lucky escape, my friend...

One in three marriages end in divorce and that's without counting the number that carry on in faithless misery...

Truthfully, she wasn't good at broken relationship counselling.

When friends' relationships broke down her standard support offering was a girls' night in. Or out. Either evening featured copious volumes of good wine combined with a boosting talk about the benefits of being single. By the time the evening was over they were generally talking about lucky escapes and exciting futures. If the malaise continued she dragged them shoe shopping, used her connections to get them a discount on a dreamy hotel in an exotic location and pointed out all the things they could do single that they couldn't do as a couple. Unfortunately she had nothing in her armoury to prepare her for consoling a Prince who had lost his bride.

Normally she considered herself a competent person but right now she felt anything but competent. As she strolled up to his side, his shoulders stiffened but he didn't turn.

Avery stood awkwardly, trying to imagine what he was thinking so that she could say the right thing. She knew how important this marriage had been to him. And now he had to unravel what could only be described as a mess. Despite that, he'd treated Kalila with patience and kindness—probably more kindness than she'd been shown in her life before.

The girl was a fool, Avery thought savagely, tilting her head back and staring up at the perfect blue of the desert sky. For someone dreaming of happy endings as Kalila clearly was, she couldn't have done better than Mal.

Slowly, she turned her head to look at him, her gaze resting on the strong, proud lines of his handsome face. Not knowing what to do, she lifted her hand, hesitated, and then placed it on his shoulder, feeling the tension in the muscle under her fingers. 'I'm sorry. I know how upset you are. And I'm sorry I couldn't fix it.'

'But you had to keep trying.' His voice was harsh and she blinked, taken aback by his tone.

'Er…yes. *Obviously* I was trying to persuade her to change her mind.'

'Then let's just be grateful you didn't succeed.'

'Grateful?' Avery let her hand fall from his shoulder. 'But you *wanted* this marriage! I know you wanted this marriage.'

He turned his head and the look in his eyes made her heart stutter in her chest. His mouth twisted into a cynical smile as he observed her reaction. 'You consider yourself an expert on what I want, *habibti*?'

The look in his eyes confused her. Were they still talking about Kalila? 'You have a wedding planned. We've just chased across a desert to find your bride. It seems reasonable to assume this is what you wanted and yet now that she's broken it off you're not putting up a fight and you don't seem remotely heartbroken.'

There was a strange light in his eyes. 'Heartbroken?'

Exasperated and confused by his lack of emotion, Avery held back her temper. 'OK, so obviously you're *not* heartbroken because you don't have a heart. Silly me.'

'You think I don't have a heart?' Under the sweep of thick dark lashes, something dangerous lurked in his eyes and Avery felt as if she'd just jumped into the ocean and found herself way out of her depth.

How had she ever become trapped in this conversation? They were supposed to be talking about Kalila.

'All I know is that you don't seem to be fighting to keep her. Is it pride?' And she knew all about that, didn't she? 'Because honestly I think you should try and get over that. She's perfect for you in so many ways. Go back in there now, give that muscle-bound wimp his marching orders— and by the way, she needs a new bodyguard because that one *definitely* isn't fit for purpose—and talk some sense into her.'

Her words were greeted by a prolonged silence.

Just when it was becoming awkward, he breathed deeply. 'Are you really that desperate to see me married to someone else?'

'Yes—' Her heart was bumping and she trod through the conversation like someone walking on quicksand. 'Yes, I am.'

There was a hard, humourless slant to his smile. 'Would that make it easier?'

It would have been a waste of time to pretend she didn't know what he was talking about. Their eyes locked for a brief moment but it was long enough for her to know that she was in trouble. 'Let's not do this, Mal.'

But of course he didn't listen. His hand slid beneath her chin and he forced her to look at him. 'We're doing this.' This time his tone was harsh. 'We've wasted enough time and taken enough wrong turnings. Just because we made a mistake once doesn't mean we have to do it again.'

'For crying out loud—' the words were shaky '—five minutes ago you were engaged to marry another woman.'

'That wasn't my choice. This is.'

That didn't make sense to her. Despite duty and responsibility, he was a man who chose his own path.

'What the hell are you saying? Mal—'

'Tell me why you were so determined that I marry Kalila. Tell me, Avery. Spell it out.'

'Because you're the marrying type and because she's perfect for you and because—' she choked on the confession '—and because I thought it would make it easier if you were married.'

Emotion flared in his eyes. 'And did it?'

'No.' The words came out as a whisper. 'No. It didn't. Nothing does. But that doesn't stop me hoping and trying.'

'You don't have to do either.'

Yes, she did. 'Nothing has changed, Mal—'

That clearly wasn't the answer he wanted and he looked away for a moment, jaw tense. 'No? If that's true then it's just because you are the most stubborn woman I've ever met. But I can be stubborn too.' Without giving her a chance to respond, he closed his hand over hers and pulled his phone out of his pocket. After a brief one-way conversation during which he delivered what sounded like a volley of instructions in his own language, he hung up. 'Is there anything in your bag that you need? Because if there is, tell me now.'

'Need for what? Who were you phoning?'

'Rafiq. You remember my Chief Adviser?'

'Of course. I love him. I would have offered him a job on my team if I'd thought there was any chance that he'd leave you. So what completely unreasonable request have you placed in the poor man's lap this time?' As the words left her mouth she heard the sound of a helicopter approach and looked up, her brows lifting as she saw the Sultan's insignia. 'I see you and discretion have parted company.'

'There is no longer a need for discretion. There is, however, a need to get the next part of the journey over as fast as possible.'

'You're leaving in style, Mal, I have to hand you that.'

'*We're* leaving in style.' His grip on her hand tightened. 'You're coming with me.'

It was a command, not a question.

Avery's heart stumbled but whether that was because of his unexpected words or the feel of his fingers locked with hers, she wasn't sure. 'What about Kalila?'

'Can we *stop* talking about Kalila?' His tone was raw. 'She has my protection and I will do my best for her, but right now I don't want to waste any more time thinking about it.'

'I really ought to get back to London. I have the Senator's party to run and I can't just take time off.'

'Of course you can. You're the boss. You can do whatever you like. Call Jenny and put her in charge for a few days.'

'I couldn't possibly do that.' Her mouth was dry and her heart was pounding. 'It's out of the question.'

'Really? The advice you give others is to face your fears—' ebony eyes glittered dark with mockery '—and yet I don't see you facing yours.'

'There's nothing to face. I'm not afraid.'

'Yes, you are. You're terrified. So terrified that your hands are shaking.'

'You're wrong.' She stuffed her hands in her pockets. 'So if you're such an expert you'd better tell me what it is I'm supposedly afraid of.'

'Me,' he said softly. 'You're afraid to be alone with me.'

CHAPTER SIX

MAL was braced for her to throw a million arguments why she couldn't do this but she simply lifted her chin in the air and walked briskly by his side to the helicopter and he allowed himself a smile because although she would have hated to admit it, she was totally predictable. Because he'd challenged her, she just had to prove him wrong.

As the ever loyal Rafiq appeared, Mal delivered a series of succinct instructions, threw him the keys to the vehicle and followed Avery into the helicopter.

There were a million things that demanded his attention, but only one that he cared about right at that moment.

And suddenly he was grateful for her pride and stubbornness because it was only those two things that had her stepping into his helicopter without an argument. It was pride that kept that back straight as she settled into her seat, pride that had her greeting his pilot with her usual warm smile and no visible evidence of tension.

As the doors closed, she turned to him, her gaze cool. 'So here I am. By your side and unafraid. Sorry to disappoint you. You've lost.'

'I'm not disappointed.' And he certainly hadn't lost.

'So where are we going?'

'Somewhere we can be sure of privacy.' He watched as

her shoulders shifted defensively and her mouth tightened as she instinctively recoiled from the threat of intimacy.

'I'm surprised you don't just want to return to the palace. Your wedding plans have fallen apart. Shouldn't you be talking to your father?'

'I've already spoken to him. I told him I will be back in a few days and we can discuss it further then.'

'I would have thought the cancellation of your marriage would have taken precedence over everything else.'

'Not everything.' Not *this*. The most important thing of all.

He realised now how badly he'd got it wrong. He, who prided himself on his negotiation skills, had made so many fundamental errors with this woman who was so unlike any other woman.

He'd been complacent. Sure of himself. Sure of *her*.

It wasn't a mistake he was going to make again.

The helicopter rose into the air and neither of them spoke again during the forty-minute journey. And then he saw the change in her as she finally realised their destination. 'The Zubran Desert Spa?'

She'd used it as a venue for an event a while back. It had been the place they'd moved from friends to something more. It had significance, marking an important milestone in their relationship.

He'd chosen it for that reason. He'd wanted significance. He wanted to tear down every barrier she erected between them and when she turned to face him he knew he'd succeeded.

'Why here?'

'Why not?'

Blame mingled with vulnerability. 'You're not playing fair.'

Could he be accused of dirty tactics? Possibly, but he felt

no guilt. When the stakes were this high, all tactics were justified. He was going to use everything at his disposal to get her to open up. He was going to fight for their relationship, fight *her* if necessary, and he'd keep fighting until he had the outcome he wanted. He hadn't expected to get a second chance but now he had, he wasn't going to waste it.

'I don't play to be fair. I play to win.'

'You mean you have to get your own way in everything.'

'Hardly.' If he'd had his own way they never would have parted. It had been the first time in his life he'd felt helpless.

As the doors to the helicopter opened, they were met by the hotel manager and an entourage of excited staff.

'They've mistaken you for a rock star,' Avery murmured as she reached for her bag and stood up. 'Do you want to break it to them that you're no one important, or shall I?'

'I suggest you don't ruin their fun.'

'When a new employee starts in my office and they're overwhelmed by the people we deal with, I remind them that famous people are all human beings with the same basic needs.'

'Sexual?'

Colour warmed her cheeks. 'How typical of you to pick that need first. Others would have gone for something different.'

'Others haven't just been trapped in a desert with you for two days.' Speaking under his breath, Mal urged her towards the welcoming committee.

'Your Highness, it is a pleasure to welcome you back. We are so honoured that you have chosen to spend a few days with us.' Clearly overwhelmed by the importance of his guest, the manager of the hotel bowed deeply. 'Your instructions have been carried out precisely, but should you need anything else—'

'Privacy.' Mal's eyes were on Avery's taut profile. 'My greatest need right at this moment is for privacy.'

'And we pride ourselves on our ability to offer our guests exactly that. I will escort you straight to the Sultan's Suite, Your Highness, and can I say once again what an honour it is to be able to welcome you.'

The Sultan's Suite. The place they'd spent their first night together.

Avery tried to slow her pace but he gripped her hand firmly as they walked along the curving path that led to the exclusive desert villa. And it was no use pretending that he was forcing her. She was a grown woman with a mind of her own. She could have walked away at any point in the past few hours, but she hadn't. And what did that make her? A fool, definitely.

If only he hadn't accused her of being scared. That comment alone had made it impossible for her to refuse, and—

—he'd made it impossible for her to refuse!

Her eyes narrowed dangerously.

She turned her head to look at him, the movement sending her hair whipping across her back. 'You are an underhanded, manipulative snake.' She kept her voice low so that the manager couldn't overhear but clearly Mal caught the words because he smiled.

'Save the compliments until we are alone, *habibti.*'

'You made that comment about me being afraid because you knew I'd have to prove you wrong.'

'So does that make me manipulative or you predictable?'

The fact that he knew her so well didn't improve her mood. 'I suppose you think you're clever.'

'Desperate,' he murmured, his thumb stroking her palm. 'Desperate would be the word I'd use. Even famous people have needs, you know.'

She did know.

And the contrast between his gentle, seductive touch and the raw desire she saw in his eyes unsettled her more than words could. The heat rushed through her and suddenly she was truly afraid. Not of him but for herself. She'd spent the past months trying to get over him. Hauling herself out of bed every day and reminding herself that she was not going to ruin her life over a man, even a spectacular man. And yet here she was, about to risk it all again.

And now there was no Kalila. There was no virgin bride. Nothing to keep them apart.

Nothing except all the usual reasons.

She tried to snatch her hand from his but his grip was unyielding. 'This is a mistake.'

'If it's a mistake then I'll take it like a man.'

That offered her no comfort because his masculinity had never been in question. From the hard-packed muscle of his wide shoulders to the powerful legs and the iron self-discipline that drove him, he was more of a man than any she'd met.

'You're going to regret this.'

And so was she.

When he'd told her to drop everything and come with him she should have pleaded workload or an event that couldn't possibly continue without her personal attention. Anything that would have got her out of this situation.

But the manager was already bowing again as they reached the doorway of the exclusive villa and it was too late for her to back out.

'The doctor is waiting for you, Your Highness, as instructed.'

Mal murmured his thanks and Avery frowned.

'Doctor?' She tugged her hand free of his and pulled off

her hiking boots. It was a relief to be rid of them because they were heavy and hot. 'Who needs a doctor?'

'You do. I want you checked after that scorpion bite.'

'Oh for goodness' sake, I'm fine.'

'The doctor will decide that.'

'He might send me home,' she muttered in an undertone. 'Have you thought of that?'

'Or he might send you to bed, where you are going to end up either way.'

'You think so? Maybe you're a little over-confident, Your Highness.'

'And you are the most aggravating woman I've ever encountered. The scorpion met its match. Even now it is probably engaged in a session of psychotherapy as part of the recovery process.' Mal stepped forward and there was a brief exchange with the doctor, during which Avery tapped her foot impatiently.

'I am as healthy as a horse.'

'When I hear that from a professional I will be reassured. If you go through to the master bedroom, he will examine you. And try not to take your frustration out on the doctor. He's an innocent party.'

'You think I'm frustrated?'

'I truly hope so. But we'll talk about this later.' Maddeningly cool, Mal strolled towards the bedroom and opened the doors and her heart skidded in her chest because there in the centre was the hand-crafted bed that had witnessed the shift in their relationship from friends to lovers.

The sensual, unashamed luxury of the suite unsettled her as much as the look in his eyes.

'What's the doctor supposed to do? Declare me fit for action?' Her response was flippant and she realised that she hadn't thought about the scorpion bite for hours. She'd been too caught up in all the drama and the swirling mess of her own feelings. She'd been too busy thinking about *him*.

And he knew it.

He hovered while the doctor examined her and Avery almost felt sorry for the man as Mal subjected him to a volley of cross-questioning until finally he was satisfied.

Exhausted, she flopped back against the pillows. 'You terrified that poor man. His hands were shaking. For God's sake, Mal, ease up on people, will you?'

'I just wanted to make sure he was thorough.'

The room was the ultimate in sophistication. Decorated with elaborate woven rugs and antique furniture, the doors opened onto an uninterrupted view of the desert. Last time she was here with him she'd taken a picture of the same view at sunset and made it her screen saver. Seeing it again now made her heart lift and ache at the same time because it brought back memories of a time when life had been close to perfect.

The mattress dipped slightly as Mal sat down next to her. 'You are thinking about the last time we were here.'

'No. I don't do that sort of thing. If you wanted sentimental then you picked the wrong woman. But you discovered that a while ago.' Sliding away from him, Avery sprang from the bed. 'What I was actually thinking is that I need a shower. My hair is full of sand. My clothes are full of sand. Right now I'm more camel than human.' She shot towards the bathroom because it was the only room with a lock on the door, but he caught her easily and pulled her firmly back towards him.

'There is nowhere to run. It's just you and me, *habibti*.'

'And you only have yourself to blame for that. I told you you'd regret it.'

'Do I look as if I'm regretting it?' Smiling slightly, he slid his hands either side of her face, tilting her head. 'Do you really want to fight? Because I'll fight if that's what you want. Or you could listen to an alternative suggestion as to how we can spend this time we have together.'

'No.' The word was meant to be firm and decisive. Instead it sounded more like a pathetic plea and he frowned, the smile fading from his eyes.

'How long are you going to keep pretending this isn't what you want?'

'As long as it takes for you to get the message. What I want is a shower.' Her voice was croaky. And she was terrified. Terrified of the thought of doing this again. Of risking everything. *Of being hurt.*

'Shower first?' He lifted his hand and freed her hair.

'First?'

'I thought you might be hungry.'

'Shower sounds good. But I don't have clothes to change into. You should have thought of that before you kidnapped me.'

His fingers lingered on her hair. 'I can solve that, too.'

'How?'

'Sometimes being a Prince has its advantages.'

Her heart was beating fast but whether it was the fact that he was touching her or the fact that he was standing so close to her, she didn't know. 'So you've been shamelessly using your position and influence to coerce people.'

'Something like that.'

'I'm not impressed. It doesn't work on me.'

'It never did. But you *do* want me. Are you going to admit it?'

'Not until all the sand has blown from the desert.'

His eyes glittered dark. 'Then I'll have to use other means to get the truth from you.'

'You resort to violence now?'

His mouth twisted. '*Not* violence. But you will be honest because I am finished with games.'

They were talking, but words were only part of the communication between them. There was the subtle brush of his hand against her cheek. The meaningful look. The sudden rapid sprint of her heart as it hammered against her ribs. It was useless to pretend he had no effect on her. That she was immune. She was as susceptible now as she always had been. And he knew it. And the fact that he knew it made her furious. Furious with herself. Even more furious with him.

Avery pulled away and stalked over to the bathroom that adjoined the master suite. She knew her way. Had been there before. But even here the memories followed her because they'd used this room for more than a shower. 'You're crowding me and I need time to think. Don't follow me, Mal.'

And because she didn't trust him not to do that, she locked the door. And then spent several minutes just staring at it, knowing he was on the other side and discovering that a locked door wasn't enough to keep the feelings away. And that was because he wasn't the problem, was he? The problem was *her*.

She stripped off her clothes, then walked into the shower and stood under the sharp needles of hot water, washing away two days of hot, sticky travelling in the desert. She lathered her hair in expensive shampoo that smelt like lotus flowers, massaged conditioner and then stood for ages with her eyes closed while the water washed over her.

But she couldn't stay in the shower for ever.

Reluctantly, she turned off the flow of water and wrapped herself in one of the large fluffy towels that were stacked inside a glass cabinet.

Then she turned and found him standing there.

'You forgot that the bathroom has two entrances. You only locked one door.'

'Another man would have taken that as a hint.'

'And you know that how?' His ebony hair glistened dark and his broad shoulders were still damp from the shower he'd clearly taken in another bathroom. He was in the process of knotting the towel around his hips. 'Have you had other lovers in the time we've been apart?'

Other lovers? The question would have made her laugh if it hadn't hurt so much. *He didn't have a clue what he'd done to her.*

She was distracted by the flat planes of his abdomen, as hard as a board and with a tantalising line of dark hair vanishing beneath the towel. 'Of course I had other lovers. Why do you ask? Did you think I'd been pining for you?'

'Be grateful that I know you're lying. And I take it as a good sign that you're trying to protect yourself.'

'Well, if you think you know so much about me, why ask?'

'Because I want you to admit how you feel.'

'Right now? Pretty annoyed. You're in my personal space.'

'You think I'm in your personal space? Try this—' He moved so fast that she didn't see it coming and before she could even murmur his name his mouth was on hers and the chemistry was instantaneous and as powerful as ever. Everything they'd been holding back came rushing straight at them. His hands were on her hips, tugging away the towel and hers were doing the same to his until they were both naked and the only sounds in the room were his harsh breathing and her soft gasps. Abstinence bred desperation and desperation had him scooping her into his arms and carrying her to the bedroom, still kissing, their mouths hungry and demanding as they made up for lost time.

'Only you can do this to me.' He murmured the words against her mouth as he lowered her into the centre of the huge hand-crafted bed. 'Only you, and this time we are doing this properly. No more encounters in the bathroom or desperate snatched moments wherever we can take them.'

She didn't care. She didn't care where they were as long as they were together and when he came down on top of her she immediately rolled so that he was underneath.

'Battle for supremacy?' His eyes glittered dark and she smiled down at him, her lips skimming his because after so long without touching him she needed to touch.

'Can you take it?'

'Can *you*?'

And it was a question she was to ask herself over and over again as he used all his skill and knowledge to drive her wild. She didn't believe in love. She didn't believe in happy ever after. But she believed in *this* and wondered how she'd survived so long without his touch and then realised that she barely had. That every day since they'd parted she'd been starving for him.

He was hard, hot and hers, and being with him again felt crazily good. So good that she was clumsy as she moved against him and of course he took instant advantage of that, rolling and pinning her beneath him.

'I missed you.' He groaned the words against her neck and she closed her eyes because hearing him say it choked her up so badly.

'No, you didn't.'

'Yes, I did. And you missed me too.'

'No, I didn't.'

'Yes, you did. Say those words back to me, Avery. Be honest.' His hand cupped her face. 'It doesn't make you weak to admit it.'

No, but it made her vulnerable. 'I missed having someone to argue with, that's true.' She made the mistake of opening her eyes at that moment and met the heat in his. His mouth curved into a slow, sexy smile of complete understanding.

'Of course, you missed the arguments and that is all. You didn't miss this—' eyes half shut, he stroked a hand down her body and she gasped '—or this—' he moved his hand lower still and this time she moaned '—and you definitely didn't miss *this*.'

This had her writhing under him but he denied her the satisfaction she craved, easing away slightly when she arched her hips against him.

'Do you realise that the only time you show your feelings is when we're in bed together?' His voice was husky and he pinned her arms above her head, holding her captive. 'Apart from the scorpion sting, the only time I've ever seen you vulnerable is when you're in my bed.'

'It wasn't always your bed. Sometimes it was my bed.' Her heart was thumping because of course she was vulnerable. Terrifyingly so, naked in every way. All of her exposed to this man who saw so much and yet still insisted on more.

'Are you going to tell me why you're so afraid?'

'Afraid?' She tugged gently at his hands but he held her firmly. 'I'm not afraid.'

'If you're not afraid then stop trying to free yourself.' His mouth trailed over her shoulder, his tongue slow and explicit as he traced her skin. 'If you're not afraid then you should just trust me not to hurt you. It shouldn't be hard.'

It was the hardest thing in the world, to put her safety in the hands of another person. To trust her heart to the one person in the world who could break it. It was too much to ask. He wanted her to surrender something she couldn't surrender. To submit to something that terrified her because she knew that whatever he gave, he could also take away.

His mouth moved lower, his tongue flicked her nipple and a low moan of pleasure escaped her.

'Mal—'

'Trust me not to hurt you.' He murmured the words against her skin, against her body, already damp from his tongue and shivering with an excitement so intense it was impossible to keep still. She squirmed and her breath caught at the feel of him, the rough hardness of his thigh and the thickness of his penis as his powerful body brushed against hers. The extent of his arousal mirrored hers and she tried to wrap her arms around him and urge him on but he held her hands fast so that she had no choice but to submit to his will.

Struggling to stay in control, to stay in charge, Avery closed her eyes and blocked out the sensual gleam in those dark eyes. As always, he drove her to the edge. Even with her eyes closed she felt restraint slip. She couldn't remember actually why she was trying to prevent this happening. Excitement engulfed her in great waves until she was drowning in sensation, the feelings of her body colliding with her fears.

His tongue flicked over the sensitive tips of her breasts, his touch so skilled that she felt the sensation deep inside her. She squirmed, her hips shifting against the luxurious sheets, but he showed her no mercy. A moan escaped her lips but his response to that was to slide his hand between her legs, to apply his expertise to that part of her that now ached for his touch. And touch her he did, those long, strong fingers shamelessly knowing as he drove her wild, controlling her response and easing back as he felt the first ripple of her body.

'No. Not yet.'

Denied the completion she craved, she moaned against his mouth. 'Not fair.'

'I want you. All of you.' He murmured the words against her mouth and she parted her lips and tried to steal a kiss but with her hands held and her body trapped beneath the powerful strength of male muscle, she wasn't the one in control. He kept his mouth just out of reach of hers, close enough to drive her crazy and make her desperate for his kiss, not close enough for her to take control.

'Mal—'

'I want you to trust me.' He spoke softly but there was no mistaking the command in his voice and had they been in a different position she would have smiled because he just couldn't help himself. Even now, in this position of extreme intimacy, he had to be in control.

'I don't trust anyone but myself.'

'Up until now that might have been true—' His fingers, placed tantalizingly close to that delicate part of her, traced her so gently, so skilfully that the exquisite pleasure swelled to something close to pain. Her body throbbed with her need for him and he knew it. She knew he knew it because she felt his smile against her mouth as he finally lowered his head to hers and gave her what she'd craved. His tongue slid over hers, bold, demanding and unashamedly sensual while all the time his fingers worked magic. And still he held her hands. Still he held her trapped and the ease with which he did it confirmed that physically he was the stronger, but she couldn't allow herself to surrender in the way he wanted her to surrender.

'Let go of me. I want to touch you.'

'No. For now, I'm the one in charge. The sooner you acknowledge that, the sooner I let you go.' His hand pushed her thighs wider and with a single smooth movement he was inside her. Deep, sure but achingly slow and gentle and that control on his part tore at the last straining threads of hers.

She moaned and he withdrew slightly and then moved again, deeper this time, his hand on her hip, controlling her movements. The look in his eyes made it hard to catch her breath and she wanted to close hers, to block him out, but something in her wouldn't allow it so the connection continued, deepening an experience that was already terrifying.

It had never been like this before. The sex had always been amazing and each time had been different but never, ever had it felt like this. Never this close. Never this— *personal.*

He'd never demanded this much from her and she'd never given this much.

She felt the strength of him, the power of him stretching her, possessing her and she wrapped her legs around him, always active, never passive and he smiled against her lips because he recognised that need in her. He knew her so well. He knew all of her and she tried again to block him out because the level of intimacy was terrifying. She was bound, not by the fact that he held her hands, but by the fact that he held her heart. If she begged him, he'd let her hands go. Physically, she'd be free. Emotionally, she knew she'd never be free. He was the only man she wanted. He was the only man she'd ever wanted and those feelings bound her to him as securely as if she'd been handcuffed.

'Stop fighting it—' he kissed her slowly '—stop fighting me and pushing me away.'

'I'm not pushing you. Thanks to you, I can't move.'

'I'm not talking about physically and you know it.' His mouth was still on hers. Gentle and yet demanding at the same time. 'I'm talking about everything else.'

'What else is there?'

'You know.'

Yes, she knew and this time she managed to close her eyes, moaning a low denial. 'You are asking too much.'

'I'm asking a lot. But not too much.'

'You don't know.'

'If there are things I don't know then it's because you've never trusted me enough to tell me. I won't hurt you.'

And she knew he wasn't talking about the physical side of their relationship. He wasn't talking about sex or anything that they were doing right now in this bed. That wouldn't have scared her. What scared her was the fact that he *would* hurt her. Maybe not now, or even tomorrow but at some point in their relationship, perhaps even when she'd started to rely on having him in her life.

He'd hurt her before...

Panic washed over her. 'Mal—'

'I want it all, Avery. Everything you've never given before. I want that from you.' His free hand locked in her hair. 'I won't be satisfied with less than everything.'

She moaned because he was deep inside her and thinking clearly no longer seemed easy and natural. In fact thinking felt impossible as he took her in a slow, sensuous rhythm that drove her wild.

'I want to know about the dream.'

'The dream?'

'Those dreams you have. Tell me—' he breathed the words against her mouth as he broke one erotic kiss and started another '—tell me what it is that makes you moan in your sleep and wake with dark circles under those beautiful eyes.'

She was dizzy from his kisses, melting and desperate from each carefully timed thrust. 'I dream about work—' she moaned as his tongue slid into contact with hers and her senses exploded '—work.'

'Work?' His hand moved down, lower, sliding under her bottom, holding her firm as he deepened his possession. 'It's work that makes you cry out?'

'Yes.' She was on the point of begging because he'd held her at this point for so long and she didn't think she could stand it any longer. She ached with need. She craved him in a way that was indecent.

'You're lying. Tell me what you dream about.' The husky tone of his voice was unbearably sexy and she wondered how he could still string a sentence together when she herself was barely able to give voice to a moan.

'Avery—' Purring her name, he sank deep into her quivering flesh and Avery lost her grip on control, every sense in her body teased to its limits under his skilled touch. As she lost control of herself she realised that her mother had got it wrong. Yes, she could be responsible for her own orgasm, but it was so much better when someone else was. And she could be responsible for her own heart too, but sharing it was the greatest gift she could give and she wanted to share it with this man.

'You,' she gasped as he brought ecstasy crashing down on them. 'I dream about you.'

Mal lay in the dark, wrapped in the scent of her and the softness of her, holding her in the curve of his arm as the rising sun sent arrows of golden light shooting across the desert. Apart from the night of the scorpion sting, this was the first time she'd allowed herself to fall asleep in his arms, as if it were somehow a weakness to do that.

And there was no doubt in his mind that she saw it that way. As if admitting to having feelings for a man somehow threatened who she was.

It was ironic, he thought, because in many ways she was the strongest person he knew and yet he understood that her independence was driven by fear as much as any-thing. Fear of being let down. Fear of hurt. She'd told him little about her past but what little she'd told him had been sufficient for him to form a picture of a life lived devoid of paternal influence.

He'd read about her mother. About the impressive di-vorce lawyer who had sacrificed everything on her way to the top. Clearly she'd also sacrificed her relationship with Avery's father because there was no mention of him any-where, and no doubt that negative experience was responsi-ble for her damaged view of marriage. He told himself that he shouldn't judge, especially given that he knew count-less men who had done the same thing. Men who had put their own ambitions before the needs of their loved ones. Marriages died. It was a fact of life.

But they'd made progress.

It wasn't much of a leap to go from 'I dream about you' to 'I love you'.

And he was confident she was ready to make that leap.

She woke to warmth and a safe feeling. Struggling up through clouds of sleep, Avery opened her eyes and the first thing she saw was bronzed skin and male muscle.

Mal.

She'd spent the night with Mal. The whole night. Not just a few hours and not even just sleeping in the same bed, but *with* him, snuggled. Joined. And after months of try-ing to piece herself back together, piece by broken piece.

Warmth was replaced by dismay. What had she done?

It was like spending a year on a diet and then taking a job in a chocolate factory and binging from dawn to dusk. She was *furious* with herself—and with him for assuming that he could just pick up where he'd left off.

Panic exploded and she tried to wrench herself away

from him but his arms tightened like a steel band, locking her against him.

'What's the matter?'

'I'm suffering a serious case of morning-after regret. Let me go.' Had he always had muscles like this? She strained against his hold but there was no shifting him.

'You're not going anywhere. If there are things you want to say then you can say them here.'

Pressed against his warm naked body with every passing second reminding her of last night and weakening her resolve?

'Let me go.'

'Never.' He didn't open his eyes and a slight smile tilted the corners of his firm, sexy mouth. 'You are running away from me yet again like the coward you are.'

'I'm not a coward.'

'No?' His eyes opened a fraction and he looked at her, his expression shielded by the thickness of dark lashes. 'Prove it, *habibti*. Stay where you are. Do not create the distance your instinct tells you to create. Last night, for once, you were honest. Embrace it. Face the fear.'

'Last night I was an idiot. And I *don't* want this! I had it once before and it was truly horrible.' She shoved him hard and sprang from the bed, her heart racing and panic gripping her like the talons of one of his falcons.

'Horrible?' His tone was several shades cooler. 'You are saying our relationship was horrible?'

'Not our relationship, no, the part when it ended.' Flustered and confused and horribly conscious that she was naked, she grabbed the nearest item of clothing, which just happened to be his discarded shirt. 'You just don't get it, do you?'

He lifted himself onto his elbow, his inky black hair flopping over his forehead. The sheet drifted down, displaying packed muscle and abs as hard as steel. 'Given that you were the one who ended it, no, I don't.'

She thought back to that time and didn't know whether to cry or punch him. 'Never mind.' The words were thickened around the lump in her throat and she pulled on the shirt, covering herself. 'Forget it. I'd be grateful if you'd do your powerful Prince thing and call your helicopter. It's time for me to go home.'

'Wearing nothing but my shirt?'

'I'll change.'

'Don't bother. I'm not letting you go again.' He was so sure of himself and who could blame him after the way she'd folded in his arms only a few hours earlier.

'It isn't your choice, it's mine and I choose not to do this again. I won't make the same mistake twice.' But she'd already made it, hadn't she? She'd already taken more than a few steps down that path. And the wounds of her healing heart were already bleeding again. And that was her fault. Despite everything, she'd allowed them to be ripped open a second time.

'Are you pretending that we're not good together?'

His lack of insight was like a punch to her belly. Her emotions overflowed. 'You don't have a clue, do you? You have absolutely no idea.' She paced to the far side of the bedroom on legs that shook so badly she wasn't confident of their ability to fulfil their purpose. 'We've done this once before, Mal, and when it fell apart it left me in pieces. I was…was broken, and helpless and utterly pathetic and… God, I can't believe I just told you that.' Turning away from him, she covered her face with her hands. 'Just stop this, *please*. I don't want a post-mortem. Last night was last night but that's it. That's all it was. One night. No more. I can't give any more.'

But it was too late. He was already out of the bed and

next to her, gloriously naked and completely indifferent to that fact. 'You were in pieces?' The light humour had gone. In its place was nothing but raw emotion. '*When* were you in pieces? Because whenever I contacted you, you were the most perfect example of someone completely together. I did *not* see a woman in pieces, I saw a woman who didn't give a damn. Until last night that's all I've ever seen when I've looked at you.'

'Well, what did you expect?' She let her hands drop and she was yelling now, completely forgetting to lower her voice and incapable of playing it cool. 'After everything I gave you, you did that to me.'

'Everything you gave me?'

'Yes.' Her voice cracked. 'With you I did something I'd never done with a man before—I gave you my heart and you sliced it up into a million pieces and served it up in public like chopped liver. *"Here, look at this everyone, help yourself."*' That confession was followed by a horrible silence. She waited for him to say something but instead he simply stared at her, his cheeks unnaturally pale.

He swallowed, although that manoeuvre appeared to cause him difficulty. '*You* were the one who ended our relationship.'

'And weeks later you were engaged to Kalila. And news of that engagement was everywhere. I couldn't go on the Internet without having pictures of the happy couple flashed in front of my face. And everyone was watching me, waiting for me to fall apart. *Everyone.* It was like being an exhibit in a zoo. Do you know how hard it was to drag myself out of bed in the morning and face the world? Because I can tell you it was hell.'

He looked shell-shocked. 'Avery—'

'And as if it wasn't bad enough, you then had the gall to ask me to organise the evening party to celebrate your wedding. You had to rub my face in it.' All the emotion that had been locked inside her for so long came flowing out, smothering her and choking her. 'And I had to laugh and smile and say, *"Of course I don't mind,"* to what felt like a million nosy people who wanted to stop and stare at our massive car crash of a relationship. It was bad enough that you asked her to marry you so soon after we broke up, but to ask me to organise the party knowing that I wouldn't feel able to refuse—' she was sobbing now, tears soaking her cheeks as she finally lost control. 'How could you do that? How could you want to hurt me and humiliate me like that? *How could you?'*

Ashen, he muttered something unintelligible and reached for her but she snatched her hand away and dodged him.

'No! There is nothing you can do or say to make this right. I've always thought that long-term relationships were doomed but with you, just for a moment, I was happy. And hopeful. And then you did that.' The words ended on a hiccup. 'And it wasn't an accident. You did it to hurt me. And you did. You *did* hurt me, Mal. And I won't let you do it again.'

CHAPTER SEVEN

MAL stood frozen to the spot, staring at the space where only a moment ago she'd stood. Stunned, he sifted through the words she'd thrown at him, sorting them in order of importance. And when he'd done that, he cursed softly.

Mouth tight, he rapped on the door of the bathroom. The door that she'd locked, of course. 'Avery? Open up. Now.'

When there was no answer, he stepped back and contemplated his options. Examining the lock, he strode across the bedroom and retrieved the bag he'd taken into the desert. The knife felt heavy in his hand and he stared at the blade, wondering if it would serve his purpose. Silently thanking Rafiq who had ensured that he was armed with no end of practical skills, he manoeuvred the knife and successfully unlocked the door.

She was huddled on the floor of the bathroom, her arms locked around her legs, his shirt barely covering the tops of her pale thighs. His entry earned him a scowl. 'So now you can walk through locked doors? Get out.'

'No.'

'It isn't enough to hurt me once? You have to do it again and again?' Her gaze dropped to his hands. 'And with a knife? Is this a new blood sport?'

He'd forgotten about the knife in his hand and instantly he put it down, thinking that he'd never seen her like this before. Never seen her with her emotions so clearly on display. 'I did not hurt you intentionally.' With the same care and caution that he would have approached an injured animal, Mal squatted down next to her. 'I didn't know, *habibti*.' He purposefully kept his voice soft and non-confrontational but that didn't stop the sudden blaze of fire in her eyes.

'Didn't know what? That you are an insensitive bastard? That just means you have a depressing lack of self-insight.'

He chose to ignore the insult because he recognised it for what it was—a last frantic defence from someone who was terrified. 'I didn't know you'd given me your heart. Until today, I didn't think you had. I thought that was a prize I hadn't won. You didn't say anything and I—' he let out a breath '—I failed to pick up the signals.'

'And you're such an expert in body language.'

'Apparently not.'

'You didn't have to be an expert.' The derisive glance she sent in his direction spoke volumes about her view on relationships. 'I was with you for a year. A whole year. What do you think that says?'

'To me it said that we were having a good time.' Mal saw the shimmer of an unshed tear stuck to her eyelashes and his heart clenched. He lifted his hand to brush it away gently with his thumb but she flinched away from him. The shirt she'd grabbed was too big for her and as she flattened herself against the wall of the bathroom it slid down, exposing one pale shoulder. Just a glimpse, and yet it was enough to force him to shift positions for his own comfort. Enough to remind him that this woman affected him in a way that no other woman ever had. 'It didn't tell me that you were in love with me. I didn't presume that and *you* didn't tell me that. Not once did you say those words.'

'Neither did you.'

Was it that simple? *Was that all it would have taken?*
'I was ready to say them. I was ready to ask you to marry
me. I had plans. And then you told me it was over and
walked away.'

'The first I knew of your "plans" was when a creepy
guy who could never keep his hands to himself rang me
to make me an offer for my business because he'd heard I
was giving it all up to walk five steps behind you for the
rest of my life.'

Mal reined in the anger, refusing to be sidetracked. 'I
didn't know he'd made an offer on your business.'

'He was taunting me because he knew how much my
company meant to me. And I fell for it, of course.' Eyes
closed, she let her head fall back against the wall. 'He understood my weaknesses better than you did.'

'And he understood mine.' His muscles protesting at
his cramped position, Mal stood up and lifted her to her
feet, relieved when the shirt she was wearing slid back into
place and covered slightly more of her.

'I thought you were Prince Perfect. You don't have any
weaknesses.' Her hair tumbled over her shoulders, softly
tangled after a night in his bed. Without her make-up she
looked impossibly young and Mal felt something soften
inside him. He'd so rarely seen her like this. This was the
real Avery, not the businesswoman.

'You think I don't have a weakness?' He slid his hands
into her hair and tilted her head. 'My weakness is you,
habibti. It's always been you. And Richard knew it. He
knew exactly what to say to cause maximum havoc. And
his plan was a spectacular success. I lost my cool.'

Her beautiful eyes were bruised and wary. 'Sorry, but
I just can't imagine that.'

'Try. It was bad.' Mal's mouth twisted into a smile of

self-mockery. '*Very* bad. You want details? Because it wasn't pretty. I lost control, just as Kalila told you.'

'I didn't believe her. You never lose control.'

'Everyone has a breaking point. He found mine with embarrassing ease. I'd planned to ask you to marry me. To do it "properly". I knew we were happy together. I knew you were the woman I wanted to spend my life with. It was an unfortunate coincidence that Richard confronted me before I'd had a chance to have time alone with you.'

She stared at a point at the centre of his chest. 'It might have helped if you'd actually included me in your plans.'

'I'm very traditional. I wanted to ask you in a traditional manner.'

She pulled away, her narrow shoulders suddenly tense. 'Yes, you're traditional. And that brings us full circle. Even if you'd managed to ask me to marry you in the conventional way, face to face, you still would have expected me to give up my business.'

It was the elephant in the room. The thing they'd never talked about because it had seemed insurmountable. Even back then, when he'd been determined to make it work, he'd seen the difficulties because it was absolutely true that to run a business like hers would require a time commitment that the woman who married him would not be able to afford.

Mal hesitated for a beat but even that was a beat too long because he saw her shoulders sag as she took that fatal hesitation on his part as confirmation of her fears. 'I would *not* have expected you to give up your business.' But he saw from her cynical expression that she didn't believe him and he sighed. 'You wouldn't have been able to work eighteen hour days, that's true, but we would have found a way.'

'A way that involved me giving up everything and you giving up nothing.'

'No. We would have talked about it. Come to some mutual agreement, but we didn't communicate as well as we might have done.'

'If that's the case then it's your fault.'

And that made him smile because she sounded so much like herself and it was a relief. 'I agree. My fault. Except for the part that was your fault.' Noticing that the shirt was slipping again, he took her hand and led her out of the bathroom, ignoring her attempts to resist him. 'Sorry, but we need to have this conversation somewhere that doesn't make me think of you naked in the shower if we're to stand any chance of actually resolving this. It would help if you could button the shirt to the neck.'

'You're thinking about sex at a time like this?'

He gave a wry smile. 'Aren't you?'

She dragged her eyes from his shoulders. 'No. You don't turn me on, Your Highness.' His smile drew a shrug from her. 'All right, maybe I *am* thinking about sex, but if anything that makes it worse because good sex cannot sustain a relationship. Good sex does not change the fact that our relationship is impossible.'

'*Not* impossible.'

'We want different things.'

'Then we will compromise. It is just a question of negotiation.'

'In other words you'll bully me until you get your own way.'

They were in the living area now, with its sumptuous furniture and breathtaking views of the desert but neither of them was conscious of their surroundings. Just each other. Avery snatched her hand from his and took refuge in the furthest corner of the sofa, as far away from him as possible.

'What time is the helicopter arriving to pick me up?'

'It's not.' He paused, unwilling to give her the option to leave but knowing that he would never keep this woman by binding her to his side. 'But if you still want the helicopter when we have finished this conversation to the satisfaction of both parties then I will fly you home myself. Fair?'

Her eyes skidded to his and then away. 'Go on then, Your Highness. Slay me with your superior negotiation techniques.'

This time he didn't hesitate. 'You accuse me of being insensitive, and I admit the charge but you share some of the blame because I had no clue as to the depth of your feelings. You never told me. You were so busy protecting yourself—'

'—something I was obviously right to do.'

'No. If you'd trusted me—if we'd understood each other better—' He felt a rush of exasperation as he remembered how much she'd held back. 'Every time I tried to talk to you I came up against this tough, competent, ball-breaking businesswoman. Nothing could shatter that shield you put between yourself and the world.'

'It's not a shield. It's who I am.'

'It's a shield. Why do you think I asked you to organise my wedding party?'

'I thought we were already in agreement on that one. Because you're insensitive.' Her tone was flippant but he saw the pain in her eyes and that pain was matched by his.

'You cut me off.' His tone was raw, his grip on control as slippery as it always was around this woman. 'You didn't even give me the right to reply. You just told me that you weren't prepared to make the "sacrifice" necessary to be my wife—a point which, by the way, hurt almost as much as the realisation that you were not prepared to fight for the survival of our relationship.'

'Relationships end, Mal. It's a fact of life. Fighting just prolongs the inevitable.'

'*Some* relationships end.' He realised just how deeply he'd underestimated the level of her insecurities. 'Others endure.'

'If I want endurance, I'll run a marathon.'

Sensing that the way was blocked, he shifted his approach. 'I once considered you the most open-minded, educated, impressive woman in my acquaintance but on the subject of marriage you are blinkered and deeply prejudiced. How did I not realise that sooner?'

'If this is an elaborate way of shifting blame for the fact that you were cruel enough to force me to plan the celebrations for your wedding to another woman, then you'll need to work harder. I am not to blame for your shortcomings.'

'You didn't even afford me the courtesy of a face to face conversation. You just told me it was over. You refused to speak to me until that final phone call, the details of which are welded in my brain.' He had the satisfaction of seeing her shift slightly. 'That's right. The one when you told me that the only way I was going to be able to speak to you again was if I booked you in a professional capacity. So that's what I did. I booked you.' He watched as the truth settled home. Watched as she acknowledged her part in what had happened.

'I didn't mean it literally.'

'Well, I took it literally.'

'You chose to marry another woman,' she snapped, 'and you expect me to believe that you were broken-hearted? Sorry, but look at the evidence from my point of view. I hear from someone else that we are getting married and that I'm giving up my job, and your response when I say "no" to that less than appealing prospect is to immediately propose to someone else. That merely confirmed everything I already knew about the transitory nature of relationships.'

It all came back to that, he thought and realised that this was the moment he should tell her the truth about his engagement to Kalila. But if he told her, it would be over and he wasn't ready to let her go without a fight. 'I believed our relationship was at an end.' He dragged his hand over the back of his neck, forcing himself to relive those horrible months. 'I thought that was it.'

'And it didn't take you long to recover, did it? If you cared about me that much, why did you ask Kalila to marry you?'

'I didn't ask her. Our marriage was arranged by the Council. That was the deal I made with my father.' That much, at least, was true. All that was missing was the detail.

'The deal?'

'I told him I wanted to marry you—' he sat down on the sofa next to her and took it as a positive sign that she didn't immediately leap out of her seat '—and he predicted that you would refuse.'

She studied her fingernails. 'Your father is a wise man, I always said so, but I fail to see how even he would know that without consulting me.'

'He met you. You'd charmed him as you charm everyone you meet, but he also saw the problems. Perhaps he saw things I was not prepared to confront. He warned me that the sacrifice required would be too great for a woman like you. And it turned out he was right. Because I couldn't marry you, it didn't matter to me who I married. So I let them make the arrangements they wanted to make.'

Silence spread across the room. She lifted her gaze to his.

'You could have said no.'

No, he couldn't have said no.

Mal felt tension spread across his shoulders. 'Why would I? I have to marry. That point is not in question. My father is not in good health and yet under his rule Zubran has achieved an unprecedented level of stability and progress. Our economy is strong, I am taking over more and more of his role and ultimately I will be responsible for the country's future. That is a huge responsibility, but one that I'm prepared for.' He breathed deeply. 'But the prospect would have been more appealing had I been able to do it with you by my side. That was what I wanted.'

Something that might have been shock flickered in those blue eyes.

She tucked her legs under her and made herself smaller. 'So now you're telling me that? Your timing sucks, Your Highness.'

'I would have to agree with that.'

'Why didn't you say it before?'

'Because you would have run faster than a stallion in the Zubran Derby.'

The corners of her mouth flickered. Her lips curved. *Those lovely lips that he couldn't look at without wanting to kiss them.*

'So you suffered when we broke up?'

'Greatly.'

'Good.' There was a gleam in her eyes. 'Because if I went through hell I'd hate to think that you got away free.'

'Believe me, I didn't. I asked you to arrange the wedding party in a last-ditch attempt to get some response from you. A small part of me still hoped that you had feelings for me and I assumed that if you had feelings for me then you would refuse to take the business because it would be too difficult for you to plan an event that celebrated my wedding to another woman.'

'I can't believe you asked me to do that. It was a terrible thing to do. A sign of a sick mind.'

'Or the sign of a desperate man.' He stretched his arm along the back of the sofa. 'I hoped that by being forced to communicate with me, eventually you would crack and admit how you felt.'

'You thought I'd ruin someone else's relationship? You *really* don't know me very well. I wouldn't touch a man who was engaged to someone else.'

'Kalila didn't want this marriage any more than I did. She probably would have been grateful if I'd been the one to back out because it would have saved her from doing it and risking the wrath of her father. And that's enough of that topic. I've had enough of talking about Kalila and the past and the total and utter mess we made of something special. I want to talk about last night.'

'Last night was last night. It doesn't change anything.'

'Last night I saw the real you. And the real you confessed that you dream about me.' Mal drew her to her feet and this time she didn't resist. 'Have I told you that you look cute in my shirt?'

'Stop trying to soften me up.' But her breathing wasn't quite steady. 'We can't do this, Mal. *I* can't do this.' Her voice shook and he realised the fragility of what he was holding in his hands.

'Yes, you can. This is one of those occasions when you're supposed to face your fears.'

Face your fears.

He made it sound so easy and yet it was the scariest thing she'd ever faced.

'You think I'd risk letting you hurt me twice? Do I look stupid?'

'I didn't hurt you the first time. At least not intentionally, and you are at least partially to blame for that fiasco.'

'It's not a fiasco, it's a relationship. That's what happens in relationships. They break. It's a question of how, not whether.' Avery pulled away from him and wrapped her arms around herself. She was still wearing the shirt she'd grabbed and suddenly she regretted not getting dressed and putting on make-up because somehow it was easier to project a different side to herself when she was wearing her warpaint. 'People start off optimistically, thinking that nothing can go wrong, and then eventually it starts to fall apart. The only unknown factor is how and when.'

'That's your mother talking. Your mother the divorce lawyer.'

'You paid someone to dig into my background?'

'No, I looked you up, but I shouldn't have had to. We were together for a year and our relationship was serious enough for you to trust me with at least some basic information about your family, although there was nothing there about your father.'

Of course there wasn't.

'Why does my family matter?' Her heart was thumping at her ribcage. 'You were with me, not my mother.'

'It might have helped me understand you. Is it her profession that makes you so wary of relationships? Is that the reason you didn't introduce us?'

'I don't take people home to meet my mother. We don't have one of those cosy mother-daughter relationships where we shop together and get our nails done.' Nerves made her snappy. 'She wouldn't have embraced you; she would have warned me off. My mother's idea of irresponsible behaviour is a relationship lasting more than a few months and

being a Prince wouldn't have earned you points. If there is
one thing she hates more than a man, it's an alpha, macho
man. You should be grateful I didn't introduce you. It was
for your own protection.'

'Do I look as if I need protecting?' He'd pulled on a pair
of trousers but his torso was bare, bronzed flesh gleaming
over solid muscle.

Distracted by that muscle, Avery almost lost the thread
of the conversation. 'All right, maybe it was for *my* protection.'

'She sounds like a formidable woman.'

'Formidable and utterly messed up. Like me, only very
possibly worse if you can imagine that. I can see her faults,
but that doesn't mean I can dismiss everything she believes
because I believe some of it too. When we broke up I *was*
a mess.' Remembering it was terrifying. Thinking about
how much she'd changed. How much of herself she'd almost given up. Just thinking about losing her business
made her break into a sweat. 'I can't do this, Mal. I just
can't. My business gives me independence. It's my life and
I won't give that up. Seriously, we'd be crazy to even think
of doing this again because the ending will be the same.'

'No it won't, because this time we're being honest with
each other. This time we're going to understand each other.
We'll find a way.' His gaze didn't flicker from hers. 'I
love you.'

She felt a lightness inside her. A lightness that spread
and grew. She felt as if she could float, spin, dance in the
air. 'You love me?'

'Yes. All of you. Even the aggravating parts.' He gave
a wry smile. 'Especially the aggravating parts.'

Avery lifted her hand to her throat. This was the moment
she was supposed to say it back. Those three words she'd

never said to another human being. Those three words that her mother had warned her always made a woman stupid.

'I—' The words jammed in her mouth, as if her body was putting up a final fight. 'I—'

'You—?' Those dark eyes were fixed on her expectantly and she felt as if she were being strangled.

'I really need some fresh air,' she muttered. 'Can we go for a ride?'

Galloping across the desert on an Arabian horse was the most exhilarating feeling in the world. More like floating, Avery thought, as she urged the mare faster. Soon, the sun would be too high, the day too hot for riding or any other strenuous activity, but for now they were able to enjoy this spectacular wilderness in a traditional way. And with Mal by her side it couldn't be anything other than exciting. Being with him was when she was at her happiest, but didn't all relationships start with people feeling that way?

She adjusted the scarf that protected her face from the drifting sand and cast him a look. 'Do I look mysterious?'

'You don't need a scarf for that.' His response was as dry as the landscape around them. 'With or without the scarf, you are the most mysterious woman I've ever met.'

'Somehow that doesn't sound like a compliment.'

'A little less mystery would make things easier.' His stallion danced impatiently and Mal released his grip on the reins slightly. 'We should go back. You'll burn in this sun.'

'I won't burn. You're talking to someone with pale skin who has an addiction to sunscreen.' But Avery turned back towards the Spa and urged her mare forward. 'It's stunning here. Beautiful. But I feel guilty. Do you know how much work I have waiting for me at home?'

'You employ competent people. Delegate.'

'I have to go back, Mal.'

'We both know that your desire to go back has nothing to do with your workload and everything to do with the fact that you're scared.' With an enviable economy of movement that revealed his riding skill, he guided the sleek black stallion closer. 'Tell me about your mother.'

'Why this sudden obsession with my mother?'

'Because when I have a challenge to face then I start by finding out the facts. Was it her work as a divorce lawyer that made her cynical about relationships, or was it being cynical about relationships that fuelled her choice of profession?'

'She was always cynical.'

'Not always, presumably, since she met and had a relationship with your father.'

Despite the heat of the sun, her skin felt cold. Avery kept her eyes straight ahead, feeling slightly sick as she always did when that topic was raised. 'Believe me, my mother was always cynical.'

'That was why her relationship with your father failed?'

She never talked about this. Never, not to anyone. Not even to her mother after that first occasion when she'd been told the shocking truth about her father.

She'd stared at her mother, surrounded by the tattered remains of her beliefs and assumptions. And she could still remember the words she'd shouted. *That isn't true. Tell me it isn't true. Tell me you didn't do that.*

Witnessing the visible evidence of her daughter's shock, her mother had simply shrugged. 'Half the children in your class don't have a father living at home with them. You don't need a father at home or a man in your life. A woman can exist perfectly well by herself. I am living proof of that. Trust me, it's better this way.'

It hadn't seemed better to Avery, who was at that age

where every little difference from her peers seemed magnified a thousand times. 'Those kids still see their dads.'

'Poor them. I've spared you from the trauma of being shuttled between two rowing parents and growing up an emotional mess. Be grateful.'

But Avery hadn't been able to access gratitude. Right then, she would have swapped places with any one of the children in her class. Her mother wanted her to celebrate an absent father but Avery had wanted a father in her life, even if he turned out to be an eternal disappointment.

She'd never again discussed it with her mother. Couldn't bear even to think about the truth because thinking about it made it real and she didn't want it to be real. At school she'd made up lies. She'd even started to believe some of them. Her dad was just away for a while—a successful businessman who travelled a lot. Her father adored her but he was working in the Far East and her mother's job was in London. She'd stopped asking for affection from her mother, who was clearly incapable of providing it, and instead asked for money, the only currency her mother valued and understood. She'd used it to add credence to her lies. She produced presents that he'd sent from his trips. Fortunately, no one had ever found out the truth—that she'd bought all the presents herself from a small Japanese shop in Soho. *That she'd never even met her father.*

And the lie had persisted into adulthood. Until somehow, here she was, a competent adult with the insecurities of childhood still hanging around her neck.

She should probably just tell Mal the truth. But she'd guarded the lie for too long to expose it easily and it sat now, like a weight pressing down on her. 'I don't see my father. I've…never met my father.'

'Does he even know you exist? Did she tell him about you?'

They were surrounded by open space and yet she felt

as if the desert were closing in on her. Avery tried to urge
the mare forward into a canter but the animal refused to
leave the side of the other horse, and Mal reached across
and closed his hand over her reins, preventing her from
riding off.

'You've never tried to contact him?'

'No. And he absolutely wouldn't want to hear from me,
I can tell you that.' Once again she tried again to kick the
mare into a canter, but the horse was stubbornly unre-
sponsive, as if she realised that this was a conversation
Avery needed to have and was somehow colluding with
the Prince.

And he obviously had no intention of dropping the
subject. 'Avery, no matter what the circumstances, a man
would want to know that he had a child.'

'Actually, no, there are circumstances when a man would
not want to know that and this is one of them. Trust me on
that.' But she didn't expect him to understand. Despite his
wild years, or maybe because of them, he was a man who
took his responsibilities seriously.

'Whatever problems he and your mother had doesn't
mean that the two of you can't form a bond. Your mother
has turned you against him and I believe that often happens in acrimonious breakups, but their problems are not
yours. He has a responsibility towards you.'

'No, he doesn't. I'm an adult.'

'At least he might be able to shed light on what went
wrong. He owes it to you to tell you his side of the story.'

'I know his side of the story.' Why, oh why, had she ever
allowed this conversation to advance so far? 'I'm happy as
I am. I'm too old to adapt to having a dad in my life now.
Oh look, more gazelle!' Trying to distract him, she waved
her arm but all that achieved was to scare the horses and
almost land her on her bottom in the sand.

Keeping his hand on her reins, Mal steadied both horses. 'You are such an intelligent woman. I cannot understand why this issue affects you so badly. You are surrounded by evidence of good relationships. Why must you only focus on the bad?'

Avery rubbed her hand over the mare's soft coat. This she could talk about and maybe if she gave him this, he'd be satisfied and let the rest of it go. 'My mother wasn't what you'd call a hands-on mother.' That had to be the understatement of the year. 'She encouraged me to be independent, so pretty much the only time we met up was dinner in the evening. Five minutes were spent reviewing my grades, and after that she talked about her work, which basically meant that I listened to a million ways for a marriage to die. Every night my mother would talk about her day because she believed it was important that I understood exactly how a relationship could go wrong. I heard about the impact of affairs, job losses, gambling, alcoholism, addictions—*lots* of those in different subsections— I heard about the corrosive effects of lack of trust, about the impact of not listening…the list goes on.' It had seeped into her, becoming part of her. 'I was one of the few five-year-olds in the land who understood the legal definition of "unreasonable behaviour" before I'd even learned to add. Do you want me to carry on? Because I have endless experience, gathered from eighteen years of living at home.'

'And did she ever describe any of the ways a successful relationship could work?' There were layers of steel beneath his mild tone. 'Did she ever talk about that?'

Avery stared straight ahead, through her mare's twitching ears.

There was no sound except the metallic jingle of the bridles and the soft creak of leather.

'No,' she said. 'She never talked about that.'

'Did you have boyfriends?'

'Yes, but I never brought them home. She always believed that most of the factors that contributed to a breakup of a relationship could be easily predicted and she wouldn't have hesitated to point them out.'

'So you were trained to spot the potential pitfalls. You don't enter a relationship waiting for it to go right, but waiting for it to go wrong.'

'I suppose so. But given that a significant proportion *do* go wrong, that's not as mad as it sounds.'

'It sounds like a shocking upbringing for the child of a single mother and it is no wonder you are so wary of relationships.'

'There is nothing wrong with being the child of a single mother.'

'Agreed. But there is plenty wrong with a single mother who chooses to poison her daughter's mind against men based on nothing but her own prejudices.' The stallion shied at some imaginary threat, leaping sideways, nostrils flared. Mal sat firm, soothing the animal with firm hands and a gentle voice.

It took him a moment to calm the animal, a moment during which she had plenty of time to dwell on the strength of his shoulders and the strength of *him*.

Only when he'd calmed the stallion did he look at her again. 'In my opinion she had a moral duty to bring you up with a balanced view of relationships, particularly given that you didn't have an example of a positive one in your own household. You spent your formative years living alongside stories of couples at the most miserable point of their relationship.'

'Yes.' It was the first time she'd truly acknowledged the effect it had had on her. 'I think that's the reason I went into party planning. The end of a relationship was terrify-

ing, but the beginning—that was exciting. I loved glitter-
ing events, the dressing up, the possibilities—'

'Possibilities?'

'Yes, so many possibilities, even if only for the short-
term. I know that at my parties, people are happy. I make
sure they're happy, even if that is only transitory. Talking
of which, I assume you want me to cancel arrangements
for the wedding party?' Her fingers were sweaty on the
reins but she told herself it was just the heat.

He stared at her for a long moment, thick lashes fram-
ing those eyes that made women lose their grip on reality. 'No. Not yet.'

'But—'

'You were the one who wanted to ride.' He released her
reins and urged the stallion forwards. 'Let's ride.'

CHAPTER EIGHT

THEY made love in the still waters of their secluded pool under the warm glow of the setting sun. Afterwards, they dined overlooking the dunes, their private feast illuminated by flickering candles.

They hadn't spent enough time like this, he thought. The madness of their lives had interfered with their relationship. It had prevented the intimacy needed to develop trust.

'You look beautiful in that dress.' He topped up her glass with the chilled champagne he knew was her favourite.

'I suppose you think you're clever for producing it in the middle of the desert?'

'Not clever, no. Fortunate. And not the wardrobe part, that was easy, but the fact that you are here to wear it.' He'd never been so unsure of a relationship. *Never so unsure of a woman.* 'I wasn't sure you'd stay.'

'The Crown Prince of Zubran not sure of someone or something? This must be a whole new experience.' Her eyes teased him and he had to force himself to stay in his seat and not rush this. Timing was everything. And his timing had been wrong before.

'It is a fairly new experience. And not one I'm enjoying.'

'You know your problem?' Glass in hand, she leaned forward, the movement accentuating the tempting dip between her breasts. 'Life has been too easy for you. Your playboy past has spoiled you. You've had it easy.'

'My father and my late uncle would agree with you, but you'd all be wrong.'

She put her glass down and rested her chin on her palm, studying him across the table. 'When has a woman ever said no to you?'

'You did.'

The humour in her eyes faded. The caution that was never far from the surface reappeared, and she sat up and dropped her hands into her lap. 'You don't like to be crossed. You like to get your own way. That's probably what this is all about.'

'That is *not* what is going on here and you know it.'

'Have you ever had to work at a relationship with a woman?'

'Is that a serious question?' He heard the irony in his tone. 'Because if it is, I think you already know the answer to that.'

Her fingers slid slowly round the base of her glass. 'You're a complicated man, Mal.'

'This from a woman renowned for keeping her relationships superficial.'

'A sensible strategy. For some reason I didn't apply it with you and look how that turned out.'

'All relationships have rocky moments.'

'Well, forgive me if I chose not to become another ship wrecked on your shores, Your Highness.' Her tone was flippant but there was a bleakness in her eyes that tore at him and suddenly he knew he had to risk more if he was expecting that of her.

'I'm sorry I hurt you. That was never my intention.'

'I'm not sure if that makes it better or worse.'

'Better. I was so in love with you.' Admitting it was

hard, particularly as he'd been raised not to share his thoughts and feelings outside the family circle. But he wanted her to be his family and he knew if there was to be any hope of that, he had to give. 'I'd never felt that way about a woman before. I'd never been in love. It scared me as much as it scared you because it changed everything. I wasn't prepared for it.'

Neither of them took any notice of the meal. The food remained untouched and forgotten on the table between them.

'I know—' her mouth flickered '—you needed a virgin princess.'

'It was *you* I needed.' His tone was raw. 'You. From the first day I met you, in charge of that enormous event and yet so cool that I could have put ice on you and it wouldn't have melted. I'd been careful, so careful, about choosing the women I spent time with.'

'Your reputation suggests otherwise.'

'My reputation only tells one part of the story.'

She toyed with the stem of her glass. 'Let's face it, Mal, you wanted me because I wasn't impressed by your rank or the size of your wallet. I was turned off by it because in the past I've found that men like you generally think they have a free pass when it comes to women. I said no. And you were arrogant enough to see me as a challenge.'

'Arrogant? You saw that as arrogance? Yes, there were women—' and he couldn't even remember them now because next to her there was no one '—but there will always be women who are attracted by wealth and the opportunity to mingle with the famous and the influential, but that's one single part of the life I lead. Then there is the other part—' he paused because this degree of honesty was so alien to him '—the part that means your choices are rarely your own and the part that requires you to serve others while forfeiting your own wishes and invariably your privacy too. You want to trust people, so you do and then you make a mistake and you learn that trust is a luxury afforded to other people. It's a hard lesson, but you learn to trust no one except your immediate family.'

She was still now, the humour gone from her eyes as she listened. 'Mal—'

'You learn how it feels to go through life alone and because you *are* alone you are forced to develop confidence in your own decisions. And that isn't easy. In the beginning you're afraid that all those decisions are wrong.' Remembering, he gave a humourless laugh. 'You wait for the world to fall apart and for everyone to discover that just because you are a Prince doesn't mean you know what you're talking about. You want to ask advice, but you don't dare because to display such a lack of confidence would be a political error. It's back to trust again, and you remember that you can't afford to do that. So you make the decisions alone and you make them with confidence and you learn not to question or hesitate because when you do, people lose faith in you. Is that arrogance?' He lifted his head and looked her in the eyes, wondering if anything he'd said made any sense to her. 'I see it more as a product of a lifetime of making decisions alone.'

She was silent for a moment. Then the corners of her mouth flickered. 'Well, that's put me in my place.' Her tone was light but her expression was serious. 'You never told me this.'

'No. And I should have. When you and I argued, I was more myself than I have ever been in my life before. I found myself trusting you.' He reached across the table and took her hand. 'Suddenly I was contemplating something I'd always thought unobtainable. Sharing my life and my future with someone I could love and someone I knew could cope with the life I lead. For once what I wanted coincided with what my father wanted for me. I made the decision the way I've made every other decision. By myself. I told my father and he was supportive.'

'You were sure of me.'

'I was sure you loved me as much as I loved you, even though you hadn't told me that. I was about to tell you how I felt and ask you to marry me—' The memory came along with a rush of frustration. 'I had the ring in my pocket on the night I met Richard and he taunted me. Implied that you and he—'

'I have better taste in men than that.'

'I know. I overreacted and it cost me the only relationship that would have worked for me.'

'That wasn't the reason.' She eased her hand out of his and sat back in her chair. 'I was raised to see marriage as something that damaged a relationship. Something that removed choice and meant nothing but personal sacrifice. Being with a man meant giving up part of yourself. I tried moving past that. Tried telling myself that it didn't always happen that way and with you I'd begun to believe it—' she stared at the bubbles rising in her glass and then back at him, her gaze frank and honest. 'But then I took that call from Richard and instead of seeing it for what it was—a manipulative attempt to break us up—I chose to let it feed all my insecurities. You can find evidence for anything if you want to and I took this as evidence that our relationship couldn't work. That you were taking over my life. Making decisions for me. You wanted me to give up my job. I was waiting for a reason to run, and he gave it to me.'

'*I* gave it to you. I see that now. I was so used to making decisions on my own that I failed to share my thoughts and that was a fundamental error to make with a woman like you. I underestimated the depth of your insecurities and I—' he gripped his glass '—I overestimated your feelings for me.'

'Maybe the first is true, but the second—' she lifted her head and gave him a faltering smile '—no. You didn't overestimate. I did have those feelings. You were right about that. But the feelings weren't enough to cancel out the insecurities.'

'And now?' He hardly dared ask the question. 'Are those feelings enough for you to overcome everything your mother taught you? Can you forget One Thousand and One ways for a marriage to die and instead think about ways it can work?'

The only sound was the relaxing sound of water that came from the ornamental fountain by the pool.

Then she stood up abruptly and walked to the edge of the pool, her back to him. *Like a wild animal disturbed,* he thought, watching in silence.

'Don't do this, Mal.'

'I *am* doing it.'

She wrapped her arms around herself even though the evening was oppressively warm. 'Why can't you leave it alone? Why does it have to be marriage?'

'Because for me there is no other possible outcome. It has to be marriage. But, unlike you, I don't see that as a negative. I love you. You're the only woman I want to spend my life with so marriage is logical to me.' He rose to his feet, careful to give her time. He rescued her chair, but she didn't sit down. Just stood there, looking at him over her shoulder as if she was deciding whether it was safe to stay. Whether she should run or not. *Hunted and hunter.*

'I am an independent woman—'

'You're a frightened woman.' He curved his hand around her waist and pulled her against him. It felt like progress when she didn't pull away. 'It's time to separate what your mother told you from what you know to be true. I love you. You have to believe that I love you. I want you to marry me.' He felt the fear ripple through her but he kept his arm round her and held her.

She placed her hand flat against his chest, as if it was essential to keep some distance even now, during this most intimate of conversations. 'You want to kill what we have stone-dead?'

'It doesn't have to be that way. It's not going to be that way for us.'

'People say that——' There was desperation in the way she blurted the words out. 'They make promises and exchange rings and believe that it's going to last, and then it doesn't. Relationships fail all the time. How can you possibly know what you'll want, or feel, in the future?'

'When you started your business, were you afraid of failing? Did it ever occur to you that perhaps it was better not to try in case it didn't succeed?'

She looked up at him and then looked away again. 'No, of course not. But that's different.'

'Businesses fail every day, *habibti*. If yours had failed——'

'I wouldn't have let it fail.'

'Exactly. You wouldn't have let it fail. That is the reason your business is flourishing in this economic climate. Because of your determination. Because when something feels wrong, you deal with it. You flex. You compromise. And you will bring all those skills to our marriage and it will be a success.'

'Marriage is different than business.'

'But the same qualities are required for both. You start with a burning passion, and that burning passion is what keeps things alive if problems arise.' He could see her weighing it up, pitting his words against her ingrained beliefs and he held his breath because he had no idea how that fight would end.

'I'm scared—' She covered her face with her hands and leaned her forehead against his chest. 'I can't believe I'm admitting that.'

'I'm pleased you're admitting that. For once you're being honest. I can work with that. Now all I have to do is get you to admit that you love me.' He closed his hands around her wrists and drew her hands away from her face so that he could look at her. 'Is it unreasonable to hope that one day you'll actually say those words to me?'

There was humour in her eyes. And something else. Something warm he'd always hoped to see when she looked at him.

'I don't think your ego needs the boost.'

He lowered his head, smiling against her mouth as he brushed his lips over hers. 'Try me. Let's see what happens.'

'We're too different. We want different things.'

'I want you. You want me. What's different about that?'

Her fingers were locked in the front of his shirt. 'You'd expect me to give up my job.'

'Not true, at least not in the sense that you mean.' He trailed his fingers down her neck, touching the diamonds she wore at her throat. *His diamonds.* 'You are a master of organisation—that is why your parties are always such a success. You can juggle a million projects at once. You have consummate social skills and you know just what to say to put people at ease. You are beautiful, poised, generous and warm. All these are perfect qualities for the role of Sultan's wife.'

'Are you asking me to marry you or are you offering me a job?'

'I haven't asked you to marry me yet. I'm leading up to that.'

'Oh.' She was trembling against him. 'So you're offering me a job. You're asking me to give up everything and in return you give up nothing.'

'Life is all about perspective, *habibti*. Some would say I was offering you everything.'

The dimple appeared at the corner of her mouth. 'You have a high opinion of yourself, Your Highness.'

'I'm sure a life spent with you will cure me of that.' Hoping that he'd judged the moment perfectly, he slid his hand into his pocket and pulled out the ring. 'Last time I did this badly—'

'If we're talking about a marriage proposal, you didn't do it at all.' Her tone was light but the look in her eyes was panic and he took her face in his hands and kissed her gently.

'Breathe.'

'I'm breathing.'

'I want you to marry me, not because I want to ruin your life, but because I want to make it happy. I want to make *you* happy.'

'Now that is arrogance, Your Highness—' But her eyes were fixed on the ring. 'Was it Kalila's?'

The fact that she would ask him that question intensified his guilt. 'I am willing to concede that sensitivity towards your feelings has not been my strong point, but even I would not be so thoughtless as to give a gift I bought for one woman to another. It belonged to my great-grandmother.' Unsure of her response to that, he paused, watching as her face changed. 'She had a long and happy marriage, so perhaps you'll consider that auspicious.'

Carefully, she took it from him, turning it so that the stone winked in the sunshine. 'It's exquisite.'

'But will you wear it?'

She hesitated for what felt like a lifetime but which was, in reality, only seconds. 'This is huge.'

'The diamond or the commitment?'

'Both?' But his words drew the smile he'd been hoping for and he took ruthless advantage of that and slid the ring onto her finger.

'It doesn't feel huge. It feels right. It fits, *habibti*. It's an omen.'

'I don't believe in omens and neither do you.'

'But I believe in *us*. And I want you to believe in us, too. Will you marry me?' He tilted her face and she stared up at him, more vulnerable than he'd ever seen her.

'Yes.' She stumbled over the word. 'But if you hurt me, I'll kill you.'

He laughed. 'That sounds fair to me.' And if she still hadn't said that she loved him, he told himself he had to be patient.

They spent two more days in the desert. Two days during which they only left the bed to swim, ride and eat. Days during which Avery was conscious of the weight of the ring on her finger. She was aware of it all the time, aware of *him* all the time. And the feelings inside her were a stomach-churning mixture of excitement and trepidation.

But already the Palace machine was rolling into action. Arrangements were being made for her to become his bride and although it made her feel uneasy and out of control, she understood. Because of who he was, it had to be that way.

'Don't they mind that it's not Kalila?'

'Turns out that there was more to Kalila than either of us knew. I'm informed that she married her bodyguard within hours of us leaving.'

'What?'

'I would have preferred she waited. It would have been easier for her to let me take responsibility, but I suppose she was afraid that her father might find a way to stop her.'

'Or perhaps she needed to take responsibility for her own decisions.' Avery understood that, but it didn't stop her being concerned for Kalila. 'What will her father do now?'

'He can't do much. Rafiq is arranging for them to come back to Zubran, at least for the time being. But I don't want to talk about Kalila right now. I promise she won't suffer for her decision.' He lowered his mouth to hers. 'I want to think about us, and if we are discussing a wedding, I want it to be ours. Talking of which, do you intend to invite your mother?' The question was asked casually but there was no such thing as casual when it came to discussing her relationship with her mother.

'No. I've told you—we're not really in touch much now.'

'Perhaps a wedding would be a good time to reconcile.'

He had no idea. 'Believe me, my mother would be the very last person anyone would choose to invite to a wedding. Not if they want it to be a happy event.'

'And your father? I was thinking that this might be a perfect time to make contact.'

'No.' Suddenly cold, she pulled away from him. 'I'll give you a list of people I'd like to invite. Friends and people from work.'

'In other words you don't want to talk about your father.'

'That's right.' Closing down the conversation, she slid from the bed and pulled on a silk wrap, knotting it firmly at the waist. 'Not all families are like yours, Mal. I wish you'd try and understand that.' Without giving him an opportunity to respond, she walked through to the bathroom and locked the door.

And this time he didn't follow her.

Was this the start of it? she wondered, leaning her head

back against the door and closing her eyes. Was this how it happened? The first crack. And then another crack, until the cracks became a rift, and the rift became a canyon and suddenly there was nothing between them but space that couldn't be bridged.

'It is *not* going to happen the way you're thinking.' His dry tone came from the other doorway and she felt a rush of exasperation with herself for forgetting about the second door, but also relief because she hated feeling the way she was feeling.

'Please tell me that your apartment in the Palace doesn't have two doors in the bathroom.'

He crossed the room to her, lean, powerful and confident. 'It doesn't, but unless you stop trying to knock down what we are building with every thought you have, then I'm going to remove all the walls and we will be living open-plan. I know which part of our conversation had you running from my bed and I won't mention it again. If you don't want to trace your father then that is your decision, but if you ever change your mind then let me know. I will use my contacts to find the truth.'

She already knew the truth but any guilt she felt at not revealing that was drowned out by more urgent feelings as he pulled her into his arms and brought his mouth down on hers.

And afterwards, hours afterwards as they lay in the darkness in sheets tangled from their loving, she told herself that it didn't matter, that it didn't make a difference, but the feeling that she was somehow deceiving him stayed with her and it was still with her when they finally landed in Zubran City.

The Old Palace, the Sultan's official residence, was a fascinating labyrinth of private courtyards, soaring ceilings and opulence built on the shores of the Persian Gulf.

Avery had planned parties in the most luxurious and exclusive venues in the world, but nowhere had left her quite as breathless as this place. The Palace was beautiful, but her real love was the gardens, particularly the water gardens that provided a cooling sanctuary from the blistering desert heat.

It became her favourite place to escape from the madness and chaos of the wedding plans, none of which seemed to require her input. As someone used to running things, it felt strange not to have a role in what was surely the biggest event of her life.

While Mal was occupied with state business, Avery flew back to London to see clients and deal with aspects of her own business that Jenny couldn't handle. Far from being concerned about Avery's marriage to Mal, her friend was delighted. Together they agreed to a few changes to the running of the business, giving Jenny more day to day control. Avery returned to Zubran knowing her business was in safe hands and feeling slightly redundant. It was a strange feeling. She loved her work and was proud of her achievements, but she knew that for her it wasn't just a means to independence, but a shield against intimacy. She'd been afraid to share herself, afraid to trust, and her mother would have said that was a sensible approach. Until a few weeks ago, Avery would have agreed.

That was before she realised how good it felt to love and be loved. And she *was* loved, she was sure of that.

Mal loved her.

How could she doubt it? He loved her so much that he couldn't wait to marry her. There was no hesitation on his part. He was so sure of himself and of her and that made her feel wanted in a way she'd never been wanted. Her mother's only contribution as a parent had been to teach her that it was better to live her life alone. She'd never mentioned the richness of a life shared and Avery was starting to appreciate the flavour of that.

Ten days after they'd arrived back at the Palace she'd taken coffee and her work down to her favourite spot and was sitting in the shade reading through a document Jenny had sent through to her when Mal found her.

'The entire Palace is searching for you.'

She closed the document she was reading. 'I wasn't hiding. I like it here. I love the water gardens. The sound is so soothing.'

'The gardens were a wedding gift for my mother. She liked the sound, too. She told me that it was the one place in the madness of the Palace and her life that she could be sure of finding peace.'

'I can understand that. It's very soothing.'

'Do you need soothing? Are you stressed?' He sat down next to her and she realised how tired he looked. Since they'd arrived back in Zubran he'd been in endless meetings, his presence required almost continuously either by the Council or by his father.

'I *should* be stressed. Marriage and me. Can't believe I'm saying those two words in the same sentence and not freaking out and running through the Palace screaming.' Laughing at herself, Avery twisted the ring on her finger, realising that it no longer felt heavy. It felt *good*.

He breathed deeply and took her hand in his. 'You have no idea how relieved I am that you're not freaking out.'

'I trust you. And I love you.' She curled her fingers around his and smiled. 'Did you hear that? I said, "I love you." And now I just said it again. That's twice in as many minutes. I'm getting good at it.'

'It's practice.'

'Not practice. Trust.' She watched as a butterfly settled on the border of flowers next to her and opened its wings to the sun, trusting that no harm would come to it while it stole the moment for itself. 'Trust is like a door. I always assumed that keeping that door closed kept you safe, but now I see that opening it can let in good things. Things I've never felt before.'

'Avery—' He seemed unusually tense and she kissed him.

'Although we were together for that year, I didn't really understand the level of responsibility you face. I didn't understand the pressure. Everyone wants a piece of you and you have to juggle so many things. I think my job is busy, but yours is stupid. And everyone comes to you expecting a decision. I see now why you behaved the way you did when horrid Richard tried to goad you. As far as you were concerned, you'd already made that decision and moved on to the next. You were decisive because you loved me.'

He cupped her face in his hands. 'I do love you. Don't ever forget that.' He kissed her and then stood up. 'These party organising skills of yours—do they extend to children's parties?'

'You want to hold a children's party?'

'My mother was patron of a charity devoted to equal educational opportunities for all. Once a year we hold a giant children's party.' He gave a helpless lift of his shoulders. 'I confess that running it doesn't play to my skills.'

Pleased to finally have something positive to do, Avery smiled. 'Just as long as you don't expect me to do a balloon release or hire fifty swans. What's my budget?'

'Change the day.' Mal faced the Council, staring at faces aged with worry and experience, faces that had been part of his life for as long as he could remember. 'Even if you shift it by a week, that would work.'

'Your Highness, we cannot do that. You know that circumstances do not allow us any flexibility.'

He did know. He'd been living with those 'circumstances' for a decade. He also knew how Avery would react if she found out what that date signified.

And then the door to the Council chamber opened and she stood there, fire in her eyes, and he knew that, somehow, from someone, she *had* found out.

Across the room, their eyes met and he stood, forcing himself to absorb the silent accusation that flowed across the room like a lethal mist.

So that was it, then. Regret stabbed him along with disappointment and frustration at the timing. Maybe if they'd had a little longer in this phase of their relationship. Maybe if those fragile strands of trust had been given time to strengthen…

He addressed the Council. 'Leave us.'

Something in his tone clearly communicated itself to them because they rose instantly, those men for whom duty exceeded all other priorities, exchanging worried glances as they shuffled from the room. He knew there would be mutterings, but he didn't care. The only thing he cared about was the woman holding his gaze.

She stalked into the room, her heels tapping on the marble floor of the Palace that had housed his ancestors for centuries. She'd come to reject him, as a small part of him had known she would—reject her role as his lover, his wife, *his princess.*

The irony was she looked regal; this woman who had turned his life upside down from the moment he'd met her walked with the confidence of a Queen.

The moment the door closed behind the last Council member, she pounced. 'In the middle of planning this party, I had a very illuminating conversation with one of the Palace staff. Were you going to tell me?'

He didn't pretend not to know what she was talking about. 'I was afraid you would misinterpret the facts.'

'That is *not* an answer. *Were you going to tell me?*'

'I hoped I wouldn't need to.'

'So if I hadn't found out, that would have been all right?'

'Yes, because it has nothing to do with my feelings for you. It has nothing to do with us.'

'But it has everything to do with our marriage, doesn't it?' Her voice was a traumatized whisper. 'You demanded that I trust you, and I did. I've never done that before, but with you I made that leap.'

'Avery—'

'You told me so much about yourself, Mal. But you didn't tell me the most important thing of all, did you? That you *have* to be married, and that your marriage has to take place by the end of the month. And it seems everyone knows that but me.' Her laugh was agonised. 'Whenever I felt doubts, I looked at the evidence to prove that you loved me. I said to myself, *He can't wait to marry me.*'

'That is true. I do love you and I can't wait to marry you.'

'But the *reason* you can't wait has nothing to do with the depth of your feelings and everything to do with the terms of your late uncle's will.'

'I made no secret of the fact that I have to marry.'

'No, but you made it sound like a general thing, not something specific. You didn't mention the will. You didn't mention that you have to have a bride by a fixed date. It doesn't even matter who the bride is, does it?' Her voice rose. 'Just any bride will do in order to fulfil the terms of your uncle's will.'

'I repeat, that has no bearing on us.'

'So, postpone the wedding. Change the date.'

He didn't tell her that he'd been trying to do exactly that. 'You don't understand.'

'I understand that I was a pawn and so was Kalila.'

'Kalila was an attempt by the Council to fulfil the terms of my uncle's will, that's true, but she was fully apprised of the reasons behind the marriage right from the start.'

'So you were happy to tell her and not me?'

'The circumstances were different. The only reason I proposed marriage to Kalila was to fulfil the terms of my uncle's will.'

'No wonder she ran.' Her chin lifted. 'What I don't understand is why you felt able to tell her, and not me.'

'I was honest with her about the terms of our marriage and I have been equally honest with you.'

'That isn't true.'

'Yes, it is.' He saw the flicker of surprise in her eyes at his savage response but he was past caring. Past hiding anything. 'My reason for marrying you was love, but because you never believed in that love, because you never believed in *us*, I didn't dare tell you about the terms of my uncle's will. I knew you would use that as more food for your wretched insecurities as you have done before, so I told myself that I would tell you when our relationship had progressed a little further, when we had strengthened the bond, when I was confident that what we had could withstand a confession like that.'

She stood still, absorbing that. Her chest rising and falling as she breathed. 'You should have told me.'

'Apart from the element of full disclosure, my uncle's will had no bearing on our future. I would have married you anyway. The timing of that is immaterial.'

'But it isn't immaterial, is it?'

'I will tell you a story and you will judge.' Mal paced to

the far side of the room and stared out of the pretty arched window that looked down on the stables. 'My grandfather had two sons. Twins. The right of succession naturally passes to the eldest twin—' he turned, watching her face to be sure she understood the impact of his words '—but no one knew who that was.'

'I don't understand.'

'There was a crisis during the birth. An obstetric emergency. People were so concerned about the welfare of the mother that somehow the midwife who delivered the twins lost track of which was born first. A matter of little importance, you might think, but you'd be wrong. Unable to think of any other solution, my grandfather decided to divide Zubran and give one half to each son, on the understanding that whichever of them had a son first, he would be the successor. It meant that ultimately the land would be united again. And that was me. My uncle had no children, so there was only me and he was concerned by my partying and what he saw as my decadent lifestyle.' His mouth twisted as he recalled the bitter exchanges they'd had over that particular subject over the years. 'My father tried to assure him that my actions were nothing more than the normal behaviour of a young man. For a short time they fell out over it, but then they agreed a compromise. My uncle agreed to name me as his successor in his will, providing that I was married by the age of thirty-two. If by that age I hadn't settled down, then the succession would go to a distant cousin.'

'Which would keep the land divided.'

'Yes. I always knew I would have to marry because it was essential that Zubran be reunited as one country, but I'd always assumed it would be a political marriage based on nothing more than economic gain. I've met many women, but not a single one who I would have wanted to spend a lifetime with. Until I met you.'

Her eyes met his. 'Why didn't you just tell me this before?'

'If I'd said to you, "I have to be married by the time I'm thirty-two," would you have listened to anything else I said? You, who are always looking for evidence to endorse your view that all relationships are doomed? Tell me you wouldn't have interpreted that as a sign I was pursuing you for less than romantic reasons, just as you are now.' He saw her shift slightly and gave a derisive smile. 'Precisely. I would have lost you on day one and I had no intention of doing that. So I kept quiet until day two, and then until day three and I let the relationship run and hoped that if you found out, *when* you found out, the bond we shared would be sufficiently deep for you to trust me. Yes, the date by which I have to marry is almost here. It matters to my father and my people that Zubran becomes one country again. And it matters to me. But none of that has any bearing on my feelings for you and *that* is why I didn't mention it.'

'And if I had said no? What then?'

It was a question he hadn't wanted her to ask. A question he hadn't even wanted to ask himself because there really was only one answer. 'I would have married someone else. When you're wealthy and well connected there is always someone who is willing to sacrifice romance for reality. And now, no doubt, you will go away and add that to your armoury of reasons why our marriage would fail. No doubt you will hear the voice of your mother warning you that a man who needs to marry is a man whose marriage is doomed.' He threw it out there and waited for her to throw it back at him, to tell him that of course she didn't think that, but she was ominously silent and he saw the telltale sheen in her eyes.

'Mal—'

He was afraid to let her speak in case this was the moment when she told him it was over. 'Has it occurred to you that your mother could have been wrong? You're not even willing to entertain the idea of contacting your father, but it might be helpful. It might shed light on their relationship. Perhaps it wasn't all him, perhaps it was *her*; have you thought of that? Perhaps she killed her own relationship, the way she has tried to kill all of yours simply by the way she raised you.'

Her face was white, as if he'd suggested something shocking.

Watching her with a mixture of exasperation and despair, Mal wondered why this was such a block for her.

Was she afraid that she'd track down her father, only for him to reject her all over again?

Was that what he was seeing in those beautiful blue eyes?

She stood still as if she wanted to say something and then she gave a little shake of her head, turned and walked towards the door.

Mal resisted the temptation to stride after her and turn the key in the lock. 'This isn't about the fact I didn't tell you about my deadline to get married. It isn't about any of that. It's about you, Avery. *You.* Once again you are looking for excuses to run. You are expecting it to fall apart, just as your mother no doubt did with your father. Are you really going to kill what we have in the same way that she did?'

Say no. Say no and stop walking.

But she didn't stop walking and he felt a heaviness in his chest, an ache that refused to go away.

'I will be there tomorrow, ready to marry you,' he said

in a thickened tone, 'because that is what I want and because I believe in us. Despite everything, I believe in us. The question is, do you believe in us too, *habibti*?'

Finally her steps slowed. He saw her shoulders move as the breath rippled through her and then she increased the pace again and walked from the room without a backward glance.

CHAPTER NINE

It was a night without sleep. She stayed up. Saw both sunset and sunrise as she sat alone in the water garden, feet bare, hair loose, tucked away in a place that no one would think of looking, apart from Mal, and he hadn't bothered.

I will be there tomorrow, ready to marry you.

But how could she do that now that she knew he *had* to get married? It explained everything. The speed with which he'd put that ring on her finger; the fact that he'd asked her so quickly after his relationship with Kalila collapsed. It wasn't to do with the depth of his love for her. It was all to do with his uncle's will.

He hadn't been honest.

Avery turned her head. Inside the Palace, lights burned as an army of staff busied themselves with final preparations for the wedding of the Crown Prince and Miss Avery Scott. Miss Avery Scott, the woman who'd been raised to believe that a woman was stronger without a man, that a life was happier, and more secure, if it were lived alone. That the only guarantees and promises worth believing were the ones you made to yourself.

No, he hadn't been honest with her. But she hadn't been honest with him either, had she?

As if on cue, her phone beeped and she found a text from

her mother. They hadn't spoken for months. She opened it—there was only one line

Heard rumour you're getting married. Don't do anything stupid.

Don't do anything stupid…

Her eyes filled. It was exactly what she needed to see. What had she been thinking? What had she been doing? There was no way she could put herself through that pain again.

Avery stared at that message for a long time. Then she slipped on her shoes. Even the tranquil sound of the fountains in the water garden couldn't soothe her.

Her mother was right.

It was really important not to do something stupid.

She found Mal sprawled on the balcony of his bedroom, apparently oblivious to the buzz of excitement that gripped the rest of the Palace. But that was because only the two of them understood that this wedding might not happen.

He took one look at her, his dark gaze sweeping over her, taking in her jeans and the casual shirt she was wearing and his sensual mouth hardened. 'So that is your decision. Thank you for not waiting until I was standing in front of a thousand guests to break the news to me.'

'I'm not here about the wedding. I'm not here to talk about us. This is about me. There's something I have to tell you about me.' She took in the roughness of his jaw and the shadows beneath his eyes. 'You didn't sleep last night either.'

'Did you really think I would? Just say what you have to say, Avery.' The chill in his voice was less than encouraging but somehow she forced the words out.

'I have to tell you about my father. I should have told you before, but it's not something I've ever discussed with anyone.' And it felt terrifying to discuss it now but he was already sitting up. Paying attention.

'What about your father?'

She could hear the splash of water from the fountain that formed the centrepiece in the courtyard beneath them. 'He didn't leave, Mal. He didn't walk out on me or abandon me. He wasn't a high-powered businessman frequently out of town, which is what I used to tell my school friends.' One by one she sliced through the lies she'd created over the years and watched them fall, leaving only the truth. 'I'm not afraid of marriage because my own parents' marriage failed. That isn't what happened.' She'd come this far but, even so, saying those last words felt hard. She waited for him to say something. To prompt her in some way, but he didn't.

He just watched and waited and in the end she turned away slightly because saying this was hard enough without saying it while looking at him.

'The man who fathered me was never part of my life. Or part of my mother's life.'

'He was a one-night stand? Your mother became pregnant by accident?'

'It wasn't an accident.' Did she sound bitter? She was amazed that, after so many years, she could have an emotion left on the topic. 'My mother doesn't have accidents. Everything she does in life is calculated. She plans everything. She controls everything. Her relationship with my father played out exactly the way she wanted it to play out.'

'And he was fine with that? He made her pregnant and wasn't interested in being part of your life?'

'That's right.' The condemnation in his voice made her nervous about telling him the rest. She paused, trying to find words that didn't make it seem quite so cold and clinical. 'But it wasn't the way you're imagining it. My mother didn't have a relationship with anyone. I don't know my father's name.'

'He was a stranger?'

'In a manner of speaking. I may not know his name, but I do know his clinic code.'

'Clinic code?' He looked confused and she couldn't blame him for that. It was hardly the first thing that came to mind when discussing someone's parentage.

'My mother used donated sperm.' It was easier to say than she'd thought it would be, given that she'd never said it before.

'Donor sperm? She had infertility issues?'

'No. No infertility issues. Just man issues. She wanted to cut the "man" part out of the deal.' She glanced at him, looking for shock, disgust, any of the emotions she'd anticipated seeing, but there was nothing.

'She struggled to trust men so when she chose to have a child of her own, she chose to have one alone?'

If only. Avery felt her throat thicken. 'That wasn't it, either. I truly wish it were. At least then I would have known I was loved by at least one of my parents. But the truth is I was another of my mother's social statements. She wanted to prove that a woman doesn't need a man for anything, not even to produce a baby, although obviously that wasn't what she told them in the clinic. She was determined to prove that she could do it all by herself, and she did. The trouble was, she forgot that her experiment was permanent. Once she'd proved her point, she was stuck with me. Not that she let that interfere with her lifestyle, you understand.'

As Mal rose to his feet, she backed away with a quick shake of her head.

'Don't speak. I n-need to finish this now or I won't ever say it,' she stammered. 'I've never said it before and it's…

hard because I'm used to being a confident person and I am confident in my work, just not about this.'

'Avery—'

'My childhood was nothing like yours. It was nothing like anyone's. Your family was close and tight-knit. You had two parents, cousins, uncles and aunts. Even when you disagreed, you were a unit. And yes, I'm sure there were huge pressures, but you shared those pressures. I'm sure that being a Prince must occasionally have been lonely but even when you were lonely you knew there were people around you who loved you. You knew who you were and what was expected of you. You *belonged*.'

He opened his mouth, but then caught her desperate look and closed it again.

Avery's mouth was dry. 'I didn't have that. On the outside my family looked fine. Single mother. No biggie. Loads of people have that, right? I hid the truth about my father because I thought it was so shaming that my mother couldn't sustain a relationship for long enough even for a single bout of sex, but what really affected me wasn't the fact that I didn't have a father, but the fact that I didn't have a mother, either. All I had was a woman who taught me how to be a version of her.'

'Avery—'

'Most of the time I *hated* her.' It was the first time she'd ever admitted that. 'There was no affection because she saw that as weakness. No involvement in my life. We spent mealtimes together, during which she talked about her work and about how lucky we were to have avoided that complex relationship trauma. And I vowed I wasn't going to be like that. I vowed that my relationships would be normal, but she'd done her job well and the only thing that was ever in my head at the start of a relationship was, *How will this end?* She taught me how to live alone. She didn't tell me how to live with other people. And it never really mattered. Until I met you.'

'Why didn't you tell me this before?' His tone was raw and this time when he pulled her into his arms she didn't resist. 'All that time we spent together—all the times I brought up the subject of your father and you never once mentioned it.'

'Because I've kept it a secret for so long from everyone. And you mattered to me more than anyone I'd ever met. It wasn't just that I was ashamed. I was afraid that if you knew, it would kill what we had.' Admitting it was agony. 'I was afraid that if you knew the truth about me, you wouldn't want me any more. You know who you are. Your ancestors are Sultans and Princes. You can trace your family back for centuries. And I'm—' Her voice cracked and she gave a despairing shrug. 'I don't even know who I am. I'm a... I'm the result of my mother's unofficial social experiment.'

He took her face in his hands and rested his forehead against hers, his gaze holding her steady. 'You're the woman I love. The only woman I want.'

She hadn't dared hope that she would hear that. 'Even now you know?' She discovered that her cheeks were wet and she brushed her palm over her face self-consciously. 'I'm crying. I never cry.' Her voice was unsteady and his was equally unsteady.

'I'm not marrying you for where you came from. I'm marrying you for who you are and who you are going to be. You are a bright, talented, very sexy woman who will make a perfect Princess. I don't care about your past, except for the degree to which it affects our future. Can you shut out everything she ever taught you and believe in us, no matter what? Or are you going to walk away?'

'Last night she sent me a text. She'd heard I was getting

married and she told me not to do anything stupid. And I realised that she was right. It *is* important not to do something stupid—' she felt him tense and, because she saw pain flicker into his eyes, she carried on quickly '—and it would be stupid not to marry you. It would be the stupidest thing I've ever done.'

He breathed in sharply. 'Avery—'

'I love you. That's why I took a risk with you the first time, because I cared for you so much. And it's why I'm here now. I was upset when I found out that you had to get married by a certain date, that's true, but I only needed a few minutes alone to realise that everything you told me made sense. And it's partly my fault that you didn't tell me because I'm so screwed up. I *do* believe you love me but when you've believed yourself unlovable for so long, it's hard not to doubt that. I love you—' the words caught in her throat '—I really love you. And if you still want me, then I want to marry you.'

'*If* I still want you?' He hauled her against him and held her so tightly she could hardly breathe. 'There is no "if". There never has been an "if" in my mind. I have always been sure. *Too* sure, which was why I messed it up so badly the first time. And I did mess it up.' He eased her away from him and smoothed away her tears with his thumbs. 'I understand that now. You accused me of arrogance and perhaps I was guilty of that but most of all I was guilty of being too sure of us. I knew we were perfect together.'

'I'm pleased to hear you think I'm perfect.' She laughed up at him and he smiled back, but it was a shaky smile. The smile of someone who had come close to losing everything that mattered.

'You know your problem? You're arrogant.'

'A moment ago I was perfect.'

'You're perfect for me.'

A warm feeling spread through her. 'I've never had that.' Her voice faltered as he kissed her. 'I don't honestly think anyone has ever loved me before. Apart from Jen. And most of the time I drive her mad.'

'Not so mad that she didn't agree to fly out for our wedding.'

Avery stared at him. 'She—?'

'My plane lands in the next hour. She is on it. She can help you get ready and she has strict instructions to call me if one word of doubt crosses your lips.'

'It won't.'

'What if your mother texts you again?'

'She can't. I dropped my phone in the fountain.' Her voice faltered. 'But I *am* afraid of messing everything up. I don't know anything about making a relationship work. Nothing.'

'There is only one thing you need to know about making a relationship work and that is that you don't give up.' His fingers slid into her hair, strong and possessive. 'Whatever you feel, you tell me. You shout, you yell, anything, but you never walk away. Never.'

It should have felt terrifying but instead it felt blissfully good. 'My mother told me that marriage was a sacrifice, but it feels so much more like a gift.'

His eyes gleamed. 'I look forward to unwrapping you, *habibti*. And in the meantime, do you think you could change into something that will make the unwrapping more fun? Everyone would be disappointed to see the elegant Avery Scott wearing jeans on her wedding day.'

She curled her hand into his shirt and pulled him towards her. 'You want the dance of the seven veils?'

'That sounds like the perfect way to begin a marriage.'

* * *

'Where exactly are we going? Could someone please tell me what's going on?' Avery was so nervous she felt sick. 'Jen?'

Her friend shook her head. 'This is one event you're not organizing, Avery. Just relax.'

'I'm not a relaxed sort of person.' Despite the air conditioning in the limousine, her palms felt damp and her stomach was a knot of nerves. 'I'm supposed to be marrying Mal so it would be great if someone could tell me why we're driving in this car *away* from the Palace and with blacked-out windows so I can't even see where I'm going.'

'It's a surprise. You're controlling, you do know that, don't you?'

'I'm efficient, not controlling. I get things done. And it's hard to get a wedding done when the groom is in one place and the bride is in another.' Just saying those words made her heart race. Bride. Groom. *She was getting married.* 'And you, by the way, are supposed to be on my side.'

'I'm on your side. You're scared, Avery.' Jenny reached across and took her hand. 'Don't be. It's the right thing. I never saw two people as right for each other as you and Mal. And I've seen a few.'

'I haven't.' Avery's teeth were chattering. 'I haven't seen any.'

'You can borrow some of mine. OK, so there's Peggy and Jim—they're clocking up sixty years. True, neither of them has their own teeth left but that hasn't been a barrier to lasting happiness. Then there's David and Pamela—' Jenny ticked them off on her fingers '—a happier couple you never did meet. And Rose and Michael—they just celebrated sixty years.'

Avery stared at her, confused. 'What are you talking about?'

'I'm listing all the people I know whose marriages have

lasted more than sixty years so that you don't sit there with a list of your mother's divorce cases in your head.'

Avery moved the hem of her wedding dress so that it didn't catch in her heel. 'You *know* all those people?'

'My Aunt Peggy does. They all live in her retirement home.'

'But—' Avery looked at her in exasperation. 'What does this have to do with my wedding to Mal?'

'I was distracting you before you exploded with fear.'

'I'm not afraid!'

'Yes, you are. But you're facing your fear and that makes me so, so proud of you. And I really want to hug you right now but I daren't ruin your hair and make-up because you look stunning.' Jenny's eyes glistened and she sniffed and flapped her hand in front of her face. 'Oh look at me! I'm going to ruin my own make-up and everyone will think your best friend is a panda. You are a lucky woman, Avery Scott. Mal is gorgeous. He was the one who insisted on all this. The whole Palace has been in an uproar, changing everything on his orders.'

'Changing everything? Changing what?' Completely confused, Avery realised that the car had stopped. 'Where are we?'

The door opened and Rafiq stood there. 'Welcome. Can I help you with your dress, Your Highness?'

'I'm not Your Highness yet, Rafiq, but thank you.' With Jenny helping, Avery stepped out of the air-conditioned limo and gasped. 'The desert?' She blinked in the blaze of the sun. For a moment she just stood, overwhelmed by the savage beauty of the golden landscape. She never grew tired of looking at it. Never. 'But the wedding was going to take place at the Palace.'

'But you love the desert,' Rafiq said quietly. 'Although this has to be a public affair, His Highness was insistent that it should also be personal. The wedding itself is for the people, but this part—this is for you. '

Avery heard Jenny sniff but she ignored her. 'But...oh... isn't everyone angry that they had to come to the desert and stand in the heat?'

'Angry that their future Queen loves their country as they do?' Rafiq gave an indulgent smile. 'I hardly think so. And now everyone is waiting for you. Are you ready?'

Avery stared at the sea of faces. She was used to large gatherings, but never one where the attention was focused on her. She felt a sudden rush of nerves. 'Where's Mal?'

'I'm right here.' He was standing behind her, stunningly handsome in flowing robes, his eyes gleaming dark and the smile on his face intended only for her.

Even the unflappable Rafiq was shocked. 'Your Highness! Convention states that—'

'I don't care about convention, I care about my bride.' Mal took her hand in his and lifted it to his lips, his eyes holding hers. 'Are you afraid, *habibti*?'

She should be.

She was giving him everything. Her love, her trust and her heart. But the moment she'd seen him standing there, she'd been sure and the feeling filled her and warmed her. 'I'm not afraid. I can't believe you did this for me.'

'I couldn't change the date, but I could change the place.' The words were for her and her alone. He managed to create intimacy despite the crowd watching and waiting. 'Are you pleased that we're marrying in the desert?'

'Yes. You know I love it. I had our picture on the computer. It was the first thing I saw in the morning.'

'I did the same. And every time I saw that picture I dreamed of this moment.'

Her eyes filled and she gave a strangled laugh. '*Don't* make me cry!'

'Never.' As he lowered his head towards her, she closed her eyes and lifted her mouth to his but Jenny gave a shriek and intervened.

'What are you *doing*? You can't kiss her! You'll mess up her make-up and she'll look terrible in the photographs. Stop it, the pair of you. Rafiq, *do* something.'

'Sadly, it seems I am powerless, madam. A fact I have long suspected.' But there was humour in his voice as he bowed to Jenny. 'May I escort you to your seat? The others are already waiting.'

'Others?' Avery glanced at Mal. 'Who? I don't have family.'

'But you have friends.' He spoke softly, his eyes gentle. 'Many, *many* friends, all of whom want to wish you well and would not miss this, the most important party of your life.'

She glanced through the crowd of people, now silent and curious, and saw faces she knew. So many faces. All smiling at her.

'You have some seriously cool friends, I'll give you that,' Jenny muttered under her breath. 'Chloe is probably going to pass out.'

Mal smiled. 'Chloe has already passed out. Twice. I have someone looking out for her.'

Jenny glanced at Avery in despair. 'She passed out last week at the Senator's party. Which was a great success, by the way. The doves were sweet. I hope you're having doves.'

'We will have doves for our fiftieth anniversary,' Mal breathed, 'and now, if no one objects, I'd like to marry the woman I love in the company of the people who love her.'

'Can we walk up there together?' Avery slipped her hand in his and he smiled down at her.

'I would have it no other way, *habibti.*'

Rafiq looked desperate. 'But Your Highness, tradition states that the bride should be brought to the groom. That is how the marriage begins.'

'Not this marriage.' His voice was deep and sure. 'This marriage begins the way it will continue. With the bride and groom side by side as equals. Are you ready?'

Avery smiled. 'I've never been more ready for anything in my life.'

* * * * *

COMING NEXT MONTH from Harlequin Presents®
AVAILABLE DECEMBER 18, 2012

#3107 A RING TO SECURE HIS HEIR
Lynne Graham
Tycoon Alexius is on a mission to uncover office-cleaner Rosie Gray's secrets, but getting up close and personal has consequences!

#3108 THE RUTHLESS CALEB WILDE
The Wilde Brothers
Sandra Marton
When Caleb Wilde's night of unrivalled passion with Sage Dalton results in an unexpected gift, he stops at nothing to claim it!

#3109 BEHOLDEN TO THE THRONE
Empire of the Sands
Carol Marinelli
Outspoken nanny Amy Bannester may be suitable for Sheikh Emir's bed, but the rules of the crown forbid her to be his bride.

#3110 THE INCORRIGIBLE PLAYBOY
The Legendary Finn Brothers
Emma Darcy
Legendary billionaire Harry Finn is formidable in business and devastating in the bedroom. What he wants, he gets... Top of his list? Secretary Elizabeth Flippence!

#3111 BENEATH THE VEIL OF PARADISE
The Bryants: Powerful & Proud
Kate Hewitt
A passionate affair on a desert island wasn't top of Millie Lang's to-do list; but one look at Chase Bryant has her thinking again!

#3112 AT HIS MAJESTY'S REQUEST
The Call of Duty
Maisey Yates
Will tempting matchmaker Jessica agree to Prince Drakos's request? Share his bed before he takes a *suitable* wife?

You can find more information on upcoming Harlequin® titles, free excerpts and more at www.Harlequin.com.

HPCNM1212

REQUEST YOUR FREE BOOKS!

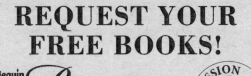

Harlequin *Presents*®

PASSION
GUARANTEED
SEDUCTION

2 FREE NOVELS PLUS
2 FREE GIFTS!

YES! Please send me 2 FREE Harlequin Presents® novels and my 2 FREE gifts (gifts are worth about $10). After receiving them, if I don't wish to receive any more books, I can return the shipping statement marked "cancel." If I don't cancel, I will receive 6 brand-new novels every month and be billed just $4.30 per book in the U.S. or $4.99 per book in Canada. That's a saving of at least 14% off the cover price! It's quite a bargain! Shipping and handling is just 50¢ per book in the U.S. and 75¢ per book in Canada.* I understand that accepting the 2 free books and gifts places me under no obligation to buy anything. I can always return a shipment and cancel at any time. Even if I never buy another book, the two free books and gifts are mine to keep forever.

106/306 HDN FERQ

Name _____ (PLEASE PRINT)

Address _____ Apt. #

City _____ State/Prov. _____ Zip/Postal Code

Signature (if under 18, a parent or guardian must sign)

Mail to the **Reader Service:**
IN U.S.A.: P.O. Box 1867, Buffalo, NY 14240-1867
IN CANADA: P.O. Box 609, Fort Erie, Ontario L2A 5X3

Not valid for current subscribers to Harlequin Presents books.

**Are you a current subscriber to Harlequin Presents books
and want to receive the larger-print edition?
Call 1-800-873-8635 or visit www.ReaderService.com.**

* Terms and prices subject to change without notice. Prices do not include applicable taxes. Sales tax applicable in N.Y. Canadian residents will be charged applicable taxes. Offer not valid in Quebec. This offer is limited to one order per household. All orders subject to credit approval. Credit or debit balances in a customer's account(s) may be offset by any other outstanding balance owed by or to the customer. Please allow 4 to 6 weeks for delivery. Offer available while quantities last.

Your Privacy—The Reader Service is committed to protecting your privacy. Our Privacy Policy is available online at www.ReaderService.com or upon request from the Reader Service.

We make a portion of our mailing list available to reputable third parties that offer products we believe may interest you. If you prefer that we not exchange your name with third parties, or if you wish to clarify or modify your communication preferences, please visit us at www.ReaderService.com/consumerchoice or write to us at Reader Service Preference Service, P.O. Box 9062, Buffalo, NY 14269. Include your complete name and address.

HP11B